KISSING STRANGERS: TAINTED LOVE

A Novella
Michelle Mitchell

Kissing Strangers: Tainted Love Copyright © 2018 by Michelle Mitchell
Excerpt, Truth Is… Copyright © 2016 by Michelle Mitchell

All rights reserved.

No part of this book may be reproduced in any form or by any electronic or mechanical means, including information storage and retrieval systems, without written permission from the author, except for the use of brief quotations in a book review.

This is a work of fiction. Names, characters, places and incidents are either the product of the author's imagination or are used fictitiously, and any resemblance to actual persons, living, or dead, business establishments, events or locales is entirely coincidental. For questions and comments, please contact at authormichellemitchell@gmail.com.

❋ Created with Vellum

CONTENTS

Kissing Strangers: Tainted Love	i
Acknowledgments	v
Chapter 1	1
Chapter 2	5
Chapter 3	10
Chapter 4	14
Chapter 5	19
Chapter 6	24
Chapter 7	29
Chapter 8	34
Chapter 9	40
Chapter 10	47
Chapter 11	51
Chapter 12	55
Chapter 13	60
Chapter 14	64
Chapter 15	67
Chapter 16	74
Chapter 17	78
Untitled	85
Prologue	87
Chapter One	91

ACKNOWLEDGMENTS

Lord, I can't thank you enough for this journey and I pray that as I grow, I can use this creative mind you've given me to be used as a vessel to do Your will. I'm forever grateful.

To my husband, thank you again for being patient and understanding when I needed to focus on writing. And thank you for trying to keep me on task when I wanted to play, I love you for that and so much more.

To Jacquelin Thomas, thank you for encouraging me to start a new project when I fretted over finishing another. I never thought to write a novella to get the creative juices flowing – great idea. As always, you rock!

To Rebecca Pau of The Final Wrap, thank you for working with me to find the right cover and color to grab attention. Based on the reactions I have received, we accomplished that goal. Thank you.

To Latoya Smith and Sherri Lewis, thank you both for taking my manuscript and helping me to mold it and prepare it for release. Your guidance was amazing throughout this process.

To all my friends and family who I requested input on my cover, several times, thank you for your honesty and encouragement. I appreciate you. To LaChelle Weaver, thank you for being a beta reader and your continued support.

And to you, the reader, thank you for coming back for more and if this is your first read, I hope you'll continue on this journey with me. God bless and enjoy.

Email: authormichellemitchell@gmail.com
    Facebook: www.facebook.com/AuthorMichelleMitchell
    Twitter: https://twitter.com/expbutterflies
    Instagram: www.instagram.com/authormichellemitchell

CHAPTER ONE

BRITTAIN

IT WAS a beautiful day for a jog. For the last three years, running was the one constant in my life. One of my girlfriends convinced me to join a national running group called Black Girls Run. It was an amazing network of women and was a needed addition to my hectic world.

I pulled my Sisterlocks into a high bun and trotted over to a park bench to do some stretching before I began my trek. Piedmont Park was really busy today. People walked. People jogged. People—that looked a lot like my fiancé, Kenneth—had picnics. *Picnics*…with another woman that sure as *heck* wasn't me.

The last eighteen months of our courtship had been comparable to what you would read in a bestselling romance. He was always accessible to me. I would've never guessed he was involved with another woman. There were so many days during the week when we had dinner together, times when he slept over, and I'd even slept over at his house. I had even met countless friends and members of his family. No one ever showed any signs of discomfort being around his side-chick. There were never any signs of another woman.

My breath caught. None of this made sense to me. Kenneth

was nuzzling this woman's neck and whispering in her ear, sharing a moment just between the two of them. I couldn't believe my eyes. I glanced down at my engagement ring as I stood frozen in time. Thinking back to the day that he proposed…he seemed so ready to commit to me.

Kenneth's soft brown eyes danced with excitement. He pulled me into his arms, lifting me off the floor.

"We've got to start planning this wedding right away. I don't believe in a long engagement."

I chuckled. "Whoa, Kenny. We just got engaged. Let's take our time and plan it out."

He shook his head. "I'll give you two months to decide what all you want, and I'm going to make it happen. I have some money saved up for this occasion, so don't worry about burdening your parents. I can't wait to make you Mrs. Wallace."

He laid it on thick that day. Clearly, I had been so enamored with the notion of marrying Kenneth that I didn't realize he was sharing his time with someone other than me. As I stood there staring at him and this woman, I wasn't sure if I should be grateful to have a front row viewing of his trifling ways, or if I should be angry that he was playing me for a fool the entire time. My first instinct was to walk over and investigate the situation, but I decided I needed to do a little more investigating from afar.

Looks like they had quite a spread at their little picnic. Their basket, which was laid across a blanket wide enough for them to lie on after their meal, overflowed with deli meats, French bread, wine, and fresh fruit. They looked very comfortable with each other. They had that sitting in between his legs with her head against his chest, while feeding him strawberries level of familiarity reserved for lovers.

I guess I could say he had a type. She, much like myself, was curvy. The top shelf was fully stocked, and the back porch could seat several men. As she pushed her long tresses out of her face, I noticed her nutmeg skin tone mirrored my own. She smiled a toothy grin up at Kenneth, and he leaned down and kissed her on the cheek.

The sun beamed across his carob complexion. I used to love that face. Now I stood here wanting to slap him into a shade of black and blue. Those soft brown eyes he used to gaze lovingly into my eyes were looking at another woman in a way I thought was reserved for me. They looked as if they had blocked out the world and were in their own space and time.

I shook my head. Perhaps I was jumping to conclusions. Maybe she was sitting between his legs because he was supporting her back. Maybe she was just a friend that had ailments keeping her from being mobile. Yeah, right. Who was I fooling with that thought? The way she began rubbing on my man's inner thigh, I knew I'd had enough discovery. This was exactly what it looked like.

I walked down the hill slowly, trying to maintain my composure, because everyone knows you don't want to look like a crazed woman when confronting the man you're supposed to marry. My intention was to just talk to him, but my right hand going across the back of his head had another plan.

"Ouch! What the heck?" Kenneth grabbed the spot where my open palm connected with his dome. His eyes bucked and his head snapped back from me to his date. He nervously wiped his hand across his smooth baby face and back to the top of his head, where sweat had formed around his freshly lined, Caesar cut. "Oh snap, Brit! Uh…hey, baby. Uh, what you doing out here?"

"Kenny, what the heck is this?" I asked, pointing towards the chick who had yet to budge from between his legs. "And don't disrespect me with a lie because I hardly think you would be feeding fruit to a cousin, sister, or auntie." I paused, planting my once flailing hands on my hips. "So, what is this?"

"First of all, you should really calm down *considering* that

I'm his wife and you're his side chick," the woman spat, rising to her feet. "I knew he was having an affair, but clearly you've lost your mind and forgotten your place. Kenneth, you really need to teach your women to learn to respect the woman affording you the luxury of taking them on lavish trips and to four-star restaurants."

My eyes blinked rapidly as I looked from Kenneth back to the woman claiming to be his rib. "Your wife? So you asked me to marry you and you're already married?" I looked at them both, holding up my left hand.

This time it was his wife who was ready to explode. I stood there and watched as she lunged across their beautiful picnic spread and pummeled him the way I should have been.

"You proposed to her? You idiot! What were you thinking?"

He threw up his hands to protect his face from the blows. "Candace, stop it! The ring doesn't mean anything. I made vows to you," he says, trying to regain some control. "Besides, it's that costume jewelry stuff."

Looking down at the ring, I slid it off my finger and I tossed it at his head. *There, I got one shot in.* I realized my true love was nothing more than unnecessary trouble.

As a crowd began to form around the tussling twosome, I walked away, gradually building up my speed and doing what I did best—jogging out my worries.

CHAPTER TWO

DARREN

I HAD BEEN TRYING to get in touch with Trish for hours since she'd left the house this morning. My job was sending me to Atlanta for a month and I wanted to see if we could spend some time together before I had to leave on Sunday. I'd just started working as a physical therapy technician a few months ago and they wanted me to attend a training conference and get some on-site training from a former partner while there. It's funny how life brings things back around. We started our life in Georgia before moving to South Carolina. Now this new phase in my life was sending me back there to prepare me for another journey.

This was a change for me. It didn't pay great, but I loved the work I was doing. It was fulfilling, and all a part of my long-term goal of becoming a physical therapist. This job opportunity, while great for me, wasn't generating the type of income Trish felt I should have. She was an executive assistant at a law firm, and in our house, she was the big earner.

My career was just one of the things we weren't in sync on lately. She was always too busy to make time for me and I was getting a little tired of being put aside. I always made time for her, no matter what I had going on. Living in South Carolina, I tried to plan small getaways to the beach, but she always acted like she couldn't get away. She used to love it when I tried to be spontaneous in the beginning, but now it was a nuisance to her.

For the first year of our marriage, we were the couple other couples strived to model. We did marathons together. Traveled across the country with no itinerary other than our desire to take in local culture and find the best burger spots across the United States. It was in our second year of marriage that Trish started her new job and our quirky relationship became boring to her, and I was no longer enough. The notion of starting a family was no longer a priority.

Up until now, I allowed our relationship to run its course and remained quiet about my frustrations. Trish, on the other hand, was quick to let me know just how unhappy she was and all I did was listen and ask how I could do better. She never told me what I could do to make her happy. It was as if she didn't want to repair our relationship. I winced as I recalled the last time I attempted to get her to talk.

"Baby, what's wrong? You keep saying you're unfulfilled, but you won't tell me what you need from me."

She groaned and threw up her hands. "Darren, stop it. I'm over this conversation and frankly, I'm over this sham of a marriage."

I could feel the worry lines creasing my forehead. "Don't say that. If you were over it, you would've left me a long time ago, but you haven't because you know you want to fight for us."

She waved my words away. "Oh please, this conversation is frivolous and you need to just stop with these asinine questions. I no longer wish to continue wasting my time on this subject when you already know what my issue is with you. When we first talked about marriage, we discussed our financial situation and career goals. You decided at the last minute to leave your career as a

Human Resources Director to follow your desire to become a physical therapist." She took a breath. *"You took a major pay cut, and put all of the financial burdens on me."*

I ran my hand across my face and looked heavenward. "I told you I wanted to make a change and you said you were on board. What changed?"

She folded her arms across and chest, and rolled her eyes. "You changed. I need a man. A real man that will stop at nothing to take care of me. I desire a lavish life. I need you to be a man and take care of home. How hard is that for you to understand?" She huffed. "You know what? I'm done with this conversation. I don't want to talk about this any further. Just leave it alone."

I blew out a breath reflecting on how much things had changed. I thought by year three, we would've gotten through that relationship hump and had a couple of kids running around. That wasn't our reality though. It was just us. My family lived in Georgia, and Trish convinced me to move to South Carolina so she could be closer to her family.

Then came her friend from high school, Zachary Hollister, who expressed how he needed some administrative support running his father's company and he wanted to have someone he could trust to help things run smoothly. The salary he offered her was way more than both of us were making at the time, and I couldn't come up with an argument for why she shouldn't take the opportunity, so South Carolina became our home. I did everything I could to please her.

My mother loved Trish, but my sister, Mya, had reservations. She thought Trish came across as materialistic and I guess she had called it right. It was Trish's desire to live like one of the *Real Housewives of Atlanta* that created division in our relationship. She was brought up with a silver spoon in her mouth, but it had never been an obstacle for us when we were dating that I didn't come from money. I always figured out a way to do more with less, which use to be enough for her but things had changed.

I had a tendency to be passive, and I knew that drove Trish. Today though, I woke up and decided to be more proactive and take a chance toward building a resolution.

As much as she hated when I dropped by her job unannounced, I decided I would go by anyway, just as she was leaving for the day and whisk her off for a romantic dinner. I managed to get last-minute reservations at the Saltus River Grill here in Beaufort. Dining along the water was always her favorite thing to do when we first started dating. Hopefully, she wouldn't refuse me. I was getting pretty tired of the lame excuses.

I pulled in front of her building and found a space. I sat in the car for a second, debating whether to call or just go straight up. I didn't want to get embarrassed if she rejected me like she'd done in the past.

I looked over to my right and saw that her boss was sitting in his car. I guess he must have been taking a nap because his head was back and his eyes were closed. I got out of the car, keeping my eyes on him. Noticing his head shift, I decided I would go over to speak. Well, that was my plan. That is, until I saw Trish rise in the passenger seat, buttoning her blouse with a smile on her face. Or at least she *was* smiling, until she followed her boss' gaze and saw me standing there.

I balled up my fists and glared at them. My palms ached as my fingers dug in deep. I wanted to strangle her, heck – kill them both – but I loved being free too much to do something stupid like that. The outcome of a black man beating the behind of a white man was not going to be in my favor. I closed my eyes and turned away, but not before releasing a thunderous growl followed by a string of curses.

Stomping over to my car, I looked back over at her – at them. I slammed the door as I got in. I was fuming as my hands gripped the steering wheel so hard my palms became red. She hadn't even moved from the car to try and stop me.

Noted…

If it wasn't over before, we were on a whole new level of over now.

CHAPTER THREE

HEIDI

SIPPING a piping hot cup of ginger tea, I smiled to myself as I watched the movers putting the boxes on the truck. I turned around at a snail's pace in the living room, careful not to miss a single detail. So many memories filled this space. I loved this home. We purchased it with intentions of having a big family, but out of the three bedrooms in our home, only one served as a place of rest. One of the rooms was transformed into a reading nook and the other into a shared office.

I glanced at the piano where we often had sing-a-longs during the holidays. The bay window where Patrick, my husband of fifteen years, and I sat when he surprised me with a puppy – the Scottish terrier I had always wanted. That was also where we sat when I told him I was giving him what he always wanted, a baby boy. It was here in this place that we cried together when we lost our son to SIDS.

Losing Noah was a major low point for us. I began to shut Patrick out emotionally, and blamed myself constantly for what happened to our son. Though I crumbled, Patrick never gave up on me and remained a constant source of encouragement and strength when I felt like I didn't want to live anymore. Back then, he was my rock, but I no longer believed he was someone I could lean on, and that hurt like hell. The trust I had for him sank the minute I found evidence of another woman in our home.

Walking over to the fireplace, I allowed my hands to run across the mantel where a few of our framed photos were on display. In the center of all of the candid photos from our honeymoon in Belize, there I stood next to my husband in a vintage, lace, wedding gown. I remembered thinking how handsome he looked on that day. His thick, chestnut brown hair, olive complexion and amber eyes looked at me with so much love as we stood in front of a waterfall taking our vows. I wanted an outdoor wedding and he wanted to be near the water. We found an amazing compromise in our wedding venue. Nowadays, we couldn't even agree on where the thermostat should be set.

I took the photo down and held it in my hands. We were so happy on that day. It was such a beautiful wedding. Five years later, and our friends and family still talked about how wonderful that day was. I chuckled solemnly as I thought of how their conversation about Patrick and I would shift once they realized I was putting him out.

I sighed as the pretty, and the not-so-lovely, memories came and went. So many things had transpired in this home, but alas, change was inevitable for us. And the craziest part of it all, I wasn't scared to adapt and start fresh. The more I thought about it, the more excited I was for what was to come.

"Mrs. Dolan, that's the last of it. Is this the correct address?" The mover pointed at the details listed on his tablet, which rested atop his protruding belly.

I nodded. "Yes, that's it. Thank you. My husband, Patrick, should be there to let you inside."

I had contemplated my next move for the past month, and I finally decided to act. Patrick was not the man I married. He was conniving and unreliable. It all started when I found a hair tie in the garage with strands of honey blonde hair that did not match my coily, bronze, natural curls—courtesy of my African-American mother and Caucasian father. I couldn't assume it was his sister's hair because she was a brunette, so that theory was out. Patrick couldn't provide me with cause for why the ponytail holder was in our house or who it belonged to, and from that moment forward, I was suspicious of his comings and goings.

The humor in it all is that he actually had the nerve to start accusing me of cheating because I refused to let the issue go. If I was at the grocery store longer than he felt was necessary, he would start blowing up my phone asking where I really was and who I was with. Then there was the time he came by my job, accusing me of having an affair with a client. I was an Assistant General Manager at an extended lodging hotel, and Patrick came up on one Monday afternoon and created quite a scene.

"Patrick, what are you doing up here?"

I noticed the crazed look in his eyes and put my hand on his shoulders, attempting to block him from continuing further into the hotel.

"Where are you hiding him, Heidi?" He pushed past me. "I know you're seeing someone else. Don't bother denying it. All of a sudden, you went from day to night shift at the hotel, and then back to a normal shift. I'm not an idiot. I know something is going on."

I huffed. "I told you one of my employees needed to be out, so I swapped shifts to accommodate the needs of the property."

He chuckled. "Yeah sure, and if you think I'm leaving before I get to lay eyes on this lover boy of yours, think again."

As Patrick and I went back and forth arguing, I never saw my General Manager, Todd, coming around the corner, and Todd didn't anticipate the right hook Patrick would plant across his chin.

"Seriously! Todd, are you okay?" I asked, reaching out to

him. *"Patrick, what has gotten into you? Just go home, please. Todd, I am so sorry."*

He shook his head. *"I just knew you would choose him over me. Don't bother coming home. Just go sleaze up in whatever room you two normally hook up."*

I thought I had lost my job that day and I was very surprised when Todd decided not to press charges. A few guests overheard the drama, so of course I was mortified. It's kind of hard to maintain order and decorum in a hotel when you've lost the respect of the guests. Todd banned Patrick from ever stepping foot on the property again, which was a small price to pay considering what could have happened.

I watched as the driver pulled away from the curb and exhaled. Leaning against the door, my mental clock began to tick as I anticipated how long it would take for the movers to reach their destination – also known as the start of my new normal.

Here we go.

CHAPTER FOUR

PATRICK

I TURNED the meat over on the grill before walking back into the kitchen to work on my special rib marinade. Personally, I didn't care to have any sauce on my meat, but I knew Heidi always pitched a fit if there wasn't even an option. Not that I was cooking for her at the moment. I guess she'd got me trained.

I opened the cabinet to take out my secret ingredients, coffee and cocoa powder. I kept this private for several reasons. I didn't want anyone complaining for one, and two, it helped me keep my title as the master griller among my friends and family. I could put anything on my Big Green Egg grill and make it taste award winning. I was still waiting to hear back from the Food Network's *Throw Down with Bobby Flay*. I'd give him a run for his money.

I was grabbing another pan of meat to take outside when I heard a knock on the door. I figured our guest had arrived, so I took the ribs off and put a few pieces of chicken on before shutting the lid.

"*Oh-my-gooosh!*"

Hearing the excitement, I rushed to see what was causing all the commotion.

"Is everyone okay? What's all the fuss about?"

"Mr. Patrick," Coryn said, swatting at my arm. "I can't believe you *finally* did it. You left your wife for me." She jumped up and down, squealing like a toddler on a playground, stopping long enough to kiss me on the lips.

As she wrapped her arms around my neck, my eyes grew wide. I gently removed her arms and planted them back at her waist. I had no clue what she was talking about.

"You Patrick Dolan?" the mover inquired.

My brows shot up as I looked past him to the moving truck parked in the driveway. "Yeah, what's this about?"

"Great. Please sign here and let us know where to put your things."

I peered over the man's shoulders at the moving truck and back at the tablet he was holding. "Uh, sir, where did, uh… who is the sender?"

The man looked at his tablet and leaned in close to my ear. "A Mrs. Heidi Dolan, sir. Your wife." He looked over my shoulder at Coryn with a smirk on his face before asking, "Where would you like it to go?"

"You can put them in the garage for now," Coryn offered cheerily. "Let me open the door." Coryn kissed me on the cheek. "This is the best gift you've ever given, Daddy. We're going to be so happy together, baby. You just wait. Follow me, boys."

I could see the judgment in their eyes, but I couldn't even worry about them right now. I winced at my new reality. *Heidi knows.* Ever since she found that hair tie in the garage, she had become suspicious of me. For her to go to the extreme of packing up my things, she must know about Coryn—or worse – she knew about Coryn and the others I had entertained in the house while she was away.

Heidi was making way too big of a deal about Coryn. I wasn't interested in her romantically. My sister had taken Coryn under her wing and provided her with a job and allowed her to rent a room. Coryn was the event coordinator for my sister's entertainment company. She recruited clients and brought in business. She was an asset to my sister, and I was indebted to my sister for helping me when I put my family in a financial bind.

This whole thing was a mess.

As I stood in the doorway motionless, my eyes darted back and forth as the boxes seemed to march in one by one. I shook my head, finally realizing what was really going on. Heidi thought she was being a sly fox. No way was I going to allow her to just remove me from my home so she could bring some other man to take my place.

I always knew she was whoring around, trying to make me feel like I was paranoid. I recalled the day she got upset that I asked to look at her phone.

"You must have lost your mind. I'm not your child. I don't mind showing you my phone, but you're giving me a schedule for when you want to check it. That's ridiculous," she exclaimed.

I crossed my arms. "Uh huh, sounds like someone is trying to avoid being caught in the act. If nothing is going on, give me the phone, Heidi. If you're not a whore, you should stop sneaking around like a whore and dressing like one."

She looked down at her dress. "You bought me this dress, idiot." She threw up her hands in surrender. "You know what? I'm going to the grocery store, and when I get back, I hope you get your act together."

She thought I was unable to see what was going on, but I was competent and able to put two and two together. I followed her to the store that day. She must have noticed me because the guy she went to meet never showed up. Lucky for her, or I would've ended them both that day.

I huffed. This would not stand. She couldn't just pack up my things and not expect me to react.

"What's all this ruckus? You know I sleep in during the

day," my sister, Suzanne, roared, rubbing the sleep from her eyes. Her faded, brown hair was pulled into a messy bun and she had on a worn, baby blue robe that looked like it could use a wash.

I was at my sister's house cooking a meal for some of her clients. They would be coming by in a couple of hours to see if they could do business. I usually tried to come over to help cook and get things in place, but I stayed out of sight because the work my sister dabbled in was not that of a law-abiding citizen. I knew staying here was going to be out of the question, and to be honest I didn't want to be here. I wanted to be home with my wife where I belonged.

"She put me out. I...I've got to get over there," I stammered. "She knows. She knows something." I gritted my teeth. "Or she's trying to move him in."

"Oh, calm down. You know good and well Heidi is not the type to delve into infidelity. She's too uptight to cheat." Suzanne chortled briefly before turning back serious. "She probably knows about Coryn because you got sloppy, and with the help at that. Being just a little too friendly is what got you caught. You didn't even bother to play down your attraction to her, and didn't make sure to leave no trace of being around any other woman than Heidi. You got evidence that another woman's been around." Suzanne shook her head. "Listen, that's your home, too, and we can't afford to have any attention over there. Better yet, we can't cause any suspicions to rise over here where I lay my head either."

I nodded. "Maybe I should just go get the...you know?" I peered over my shoulder at Coryn who had reentered the room with the movers. "It really doesn't need to be over there anyway."

"Uh uh, give Heidi the night to herself and we'll go over while she's at work. I'm sure the neighbors are already being nosey since they saw a moving truck. No need to give them something else to talk about. I guess you can stay here, but only for tonight."

Suzanne was right that we didn't need to draw suspicion, but my wife was an unlicensed sleuth and it was only a matter of time before our secret life got exposed. I nodded, but couldn't shake the thought that my wife had finally lost her mind and brought some man into our house, or worse—she knew everything.

CHAPTER FIVE

BRITTAIN

I ROLLED over in my canopy bed, my hands getting tangled in the tulle as I aimlessly reached for my cell phone. Whoever was calling had better be in need of medical attention or near death and wanted to say goodbye. Everyone knew I slept in on the weekends. With trying to balance being an RN at one of Atlanta's busiest hospitals and working on my Master's degree, I hardly ever got eight hours of sleep.

After putting in years of service, I managed to finally work out a schedule that gave me some flexibility. I decided to go part-time so I could return to school. I made enough money and I had other aspirations of becoming a nurse practitioner. And then there was also the desire to travel, meet a man, and settle down. I thought Kenneth would be that man, but I guess his wife had that idea before me. She won. I folded. I had no time for drama and planned to keep living without it.

"Hello," I mumbled into the phone, scanning the room with one eye open for the alarm clock. It was six a.m. and I was livid.

"Britt, don't hang up. Baby, I'm *soooo* sorry. I never meant to hurt you. I love you and I think we should talk. What time can I come over?" Kenneth said.

If I wasn't up before, I certainly was up now and anger was my coffee of choice. It's been two days since I discovered he was a married man, which demoted me from beaming fiancé to the unknowing mistress, and I can't stop racking my brain, trying to figure out how I didn't know he was married. But then again, he didn't act like a married man. He was always readily available to meet me. I had been to what I assumed was their home at different times. There was no sign of a Mrs. – only Kenneth's raggedy tail.

I huffed into the phone. "Kenny, I'm not in the mood for this. If you're calling about your work cell, trust, it's already been Fed Ex'd to your office and your secretary has been alerted to look out for it."

I could hear Kenneth inhaling deeply. "I could've just come to get the phone." A beat and then, "Look, I'm outside in your driveway. Can you come out or can I come inside?"

I grabbed my robe off the bench at the foot of my bed and pulled it over my body as I crept towards the window and peeked outside. Sure enough, his red, Audi convertible was sitting in my driveway. He sat on the hood of the car, seemingly dressed to impress with a crisp, white button-down, dress slacks, a coffee-colored blazer and a dozen, red roses in his left hand as his right held his cell phone against his ear. He knew I loved him in that blazer. Under different circumstances, this spectacle of love would make my heart dance, but today the sight of him made me want to vomit.

"Kenny, go home to your wife. There's nothing left for you here. I'm nobody's fool twice," I hissed.

"Fool?" He laughed into the phone. "Don't sell yourself short, Sweetcakes. You need to get up on this while it's still for the taking," he said, calling me by the pet name he loved and I always secretly hated.

"I'm not selling myself *short*. I actually want more for myself, and I'm saying I have never sought out a married man and you'll be no exception. Get out of my driveway and keep it pushing to the next one, 'cause I'm not having it." I hung up.

He had a lot of nerve showing up here. I had no desire to be an Olivia Pope. A glamorized side chick made great television, but in the real world, minus the cameras, it hurt to find out you were the other woman. Seeing him was a reminder of how foolish I had been. I'm sure he thought I would see him and come running, with his simple behind.

I padded to the bathroom to take a shower, discarding the robe along the way. I allowed the water to massage my tense shoulders and drench my face instead of the tears that threatened to fall every time I thought of how he played me. I never cried over Kenneth. I couldn't bring myself to cry over someone that didn't value me.

Calling off my engagement created an emotional strain on me. All of this building towards forever ended up being a big set up for a major let down. And it wasn't like we were just a few months into the relationship. We had been dating a little over a year and he had proposed to me on New Year's Eve. Now, here I was on the eve of Valentine's Day, trying to figure out how in the hell I got caught up.

I lathered my locks, shampooing away my worries when I felt his hands around my waist. This might have put other women at pause, but I knew Kenneth's touch anywhere. It was the reason I'd given him my spare key, because I always loved when he surprised me this way. Things were different now.

I should've pushed him away. My mind willed me to kick him out, but my heart…my silly heart welcomed his touch. He stroked my hair away from my neck, and leaned into my ear, kissing me gently.

"I'm sorry, Britt. I love you. There's nothing fake about my feelings," he said. When I didn't respond, he continued. "I didn't think you'd open up your heart to me if you knew about Candace, but we're in the process of a divorce. All I want is you."

I took a step forward, putting some distance between us. If I lingered in his arms much longer, I might be dumb enough to get closure in a horizontal way that would not benefit me in my efforts to leave this man alone.

"Kenny, you should leave," I whispered and then commanded, "*Kenny, leave*." I didn't look at him. Facing him would've made me fragile and given him the upper hand. Looking into his eyes always made me feel faint. I promise I thought I heard SWV's song, "Weak" every time I looked at him.

"Are you sure that's what you want? Because if I leave, that's it," he said. "Why did you take the ring if you weren't ready to be in this for life?"

Yep, that did it. No this idiot didn't come in here all Don Juan and ask why did I took the ring if I couldn't commit.

I spun around and pushed him against the glass door. "Kenneth, if you don't get your tired behind out of this freakin' shower, you'll be one wandering, *eye-less* man." With my hand clenched into a fist, I jabbed him in the chest. "Please try me so I can prove it!"

With his wet clothes clinging to his body, he held up his hands as he trekked back out of the bathroom, soaking up the tile floor and carpet as he made his way through the bedroom.

"Make me sick, messing up my carpet. Best believe I'm sending you the bill, with your ol' trifling 'self," I yelled after him. "And leave my spare key on your way out!"

I grabbed my towel from the rail outside of the shower, wrapped it around my waist, and took another from the linen closet to wipe up the floor as I mumbled my frustrations the entire time I cleaned.

"He's got the audacity to come here unannounced. Knowing

good and well I ain't gonna tolerate the disrespect. I'm done with him, though. I hope he got the message."

Tossing the soiled towel across the tub, I finished drying off as I made my way back to my bedroom…where I found Kenneth lying naked across my bed.

"I couldn't leave out of here in wet clothes. I hope you don't mind." He propped himself up against the pillows. "Besides, we need to get some closure on this thing. And there's no better way than to make love one last time."

While he looked tempting, there was no way I was going down this path again. I walked past him to my closet and began entering the code to my safe where I kept my gun. As the cliché goes, I was .38 hot and had to grab my .38 special.

As I turned around to let him know I wasn't playing, the only thing I saw was Kenneth's butt crack and the leg of his pants flying behind him out the door.

"Works every time," I said aloud with a smile.

CHAPTER SIX

DARREN

I WOKE up the next morning to discover Trish never came home. To say I was furious would be an understatement. I called her phone and sent several text messages. She never replied or bothered to return any of my calls. Needless to say, I didn't sleep a wink. I checked the guest bedrooms just in case she managed to creep in when I finally managed to get some rest, but there was no evidence of her having been in the house at all.

I paced the length of the living room floor. Angry was not to the best word to describe how I felt. I felt dangerous and prayed Trish knew me well enough to know she need not come home now. Not to this house. *This house*. This stupid house I built for her. When we first moved to South Carolina, we had a two bedroom condo that she loved, but once she started working at the firm, she felt the need to compete. She didn't want to buy a cookie-cutter house in a subdivision full of similar makes, models, and hues. No, she wanted to be like the wives of the executives in her office.

To think I'd used the land I inherited from my grandfather to build *her* dream home. She wanted to have a four-car garage, yet we only had two vehicles. She wanted the property to be gated, no wooden fences here. Nah, she had to have an iron-rod gate like the celebrities have. The home had to be exotic. It needed to appear to be a property that could have been in Hilton Head along the golf course. The best of everything was never enough for her. She always needed more.

Walking into our luxury, state-of-the-art kitchen with its custom designed, marble countertops, a stovetop fit for a chef, and smart refrigerator, my first thought was to bulldoze the place. Everything about this house was Trish; there was little in here that represented me. I let out a curse just as Trish came strolling through the back door. I turned to look at my whore-of-a-wife to see what she had to say for herself.

She looked as if she didn't have a care in the world. Her lips were pursed and her honey brown hair pulled tightly in a bun at the nape of her neck. I would never have described her as an ice princess before, but the rigid woman standing in front of me was anything but warm. I guess both of us had changed. Gray hairs had sprouted where my dark black waves used to be. My changes were only physical – mentally and emotionally, I was still the man she loved, or at least used to love.

The tension between us was thick. Neither of us wanted to be the first to speak. I huffed and ran my hand across my head. I couldn't believe things had gotten so bad to where I would think so low of my wife. I knew I shouldn't think like that since, after all, she was my wife and we took vows. Perhaps, we could work this out.

The silence was smothering. I wasn't sure how much longer I could take this. I wanted to be the first to speak, try to see where her head was or how she would explain herself. I couldn't wait for her to step up first, so I attempted to start the conversation.

"Trish, listen, about yesterday. I just – I just…what were you thinking?"

She slammed her purse down on the island. Her icy gaze cut

through me. "What the hell were *you* thinking coming down to my job? Just gonna come around there embarrassing me. I got to work there you know."

So much for making up. "Are you seriously questioning my actions? Can't be when you're walking in here with the same clothes you had on the day before, and acting like you couldn't pick up the phone to call to tell me where you were."

Trish rolled her eyes. "Oh, grow up, Darren," she grunted.

My brows rose. "Grow up? I wasn't the one acting like some young, dumb girl out in the parking lot auditioning to be a Dyson vacuum model. Excuse me if cared enough to want to come surprise my wife and take her out to dinner. I'm such a bad husband. Get out of here with that mess."

Her eyes narrowed and she leaned in closer. "Had you minded your business, you wouldn't have to worry about what I was doing. So what now, are you upset? You want out?"

When I didn't respond, she laughed in my face. "Fine by me. I already have a spot to lay my head. Here," she chided, tossing the keys at me. "I won't be needing these. *Hell*, I don't even need anything here. My man, my *real* man, has a closet full of designer clothes waiting for me."

I held up my hand. "If you're gonna go, there's no need for all the extra dramatics. Just leave, Trish."

She nodded. Her hair fell over her eyes, highlighting her caramel-coated skin, and in that instant I wanted to enjoy her beauty one last time. But then, she opened her mouth.

"The funny thing is, you thought you were the love of my life. But the reality of it all, my sweet, naïve Darren, is you were the one on the side in this love triangle."

I smirked. I knew Trish well enough to know she was attempting to hurt me. She knew I could be passive, where she was aggressive. She wasn't like that when we first started dating, but as she started having champagne wishes, she started to act out. It was her way of testing my emotions – questioning how much I loved her. This time though, I was tired of the chess game and wasn't going to go back and forth figuring out my pawn's next move.

She was full of it and I wasn't buying into her head games. I knew, in some regards, she saw me as a weak man. For me though, her happiness outweighed my own desires. In retrospect, I guess I appeared friable. She took my love as a sign of weakness, instead of appreciating the lengths to which I would go to give her the world.

"Whatever you say, Trish." That was my attempt at a retort, but the sneer on her face started to make me wonder if she was telling the truth. I didn't have to wait long for an answer.

"I know you think I'm just playing emotional roulette, but that's not it at all." She grabbed her purse. "Zach promised to leave his wife for me, and when he didn't act right, I played my hand. So, you see, you were just the pawn I used to help him see his queen."

I stood frozen in place. I was scared of what I might do as my anger began to boil over. I didn't want to curse her out and I would never hit her, but I sure wanted to call one of my sisters to lay hands on her real quick.

"I say all that and you stand there like a mute." She shook her head in disgust. "Typical ... you know, you could really learn a lot from Zach," she said. "He's not scared to speak up for himself. I don't want a man that I can say anything to and he just takes it. I don't want a man that can't make me feel expensive. Get it together." Trish adjusted the purse on her shoulder and sauntered toward the door. She stopped short and looked at me with pity in her eyes. "You take care of yourself, Darren."

Once the door closed, I spewed out every curse word I knew. I wanted to be angry and hurt, but a weird calm came over me, letting me know Trish just did me a huge favor. I could only pray I had sense enough to take this blessing and move forward. No takebacks.

CHAPTER SEVEN

HEIDI

I BUSIED MYSELF, tidying up around the house. There were still a few items of Patrick's left behind. There were still a few dress shirts, slacks, and shoes which I'd packed up so when he came by unannounced – which I knew would be any day now – he could just grab them and go. I mostly sent his casual clothing over to Suzanne's and a few electronics I knew he'd try to come get, and I didn't want to give him any cause to return here without my summoning him.

I arranged for the Goodwill to come in a few days to pick up the bed in the master bedroom and the furniture in the living room. The thought of Patrick having a romp with some woman haunted me daily, and a slipcover would not suffice. I made a few calls and got a great deal on some new furnishing. I couldn't wait to give this old place a new look. For now, I'd sleep in the guestroom. Hopefully, there was no activity in that room, too.

I asked my cousin, Vance, to stop by the house just in case Patrick came over trying to start mess. Vance was the only person that knew about me putting Patrick out.

I was an only child and he had always been like a big brother to me. When we were coming up, he was the one who tried to protect me from the Patrick's of the world. Naturally, I called him first to let him know I was tired and ready to allow myself to have better. Vance agreed that I deserved better than Patrick, and honestly, he never really cared for him to begin with. Hearing that I was finally ridding myself of him was a blessing to Vance's ears.

"It's about time. You know that dummy doesn't know and has never known how good he had it with you," Vance said.

I chuckled. "Now hold on, Vance, it wasn't all bad. Patrick and I had some good times, too. We really did have a loving relationship. At times, I felt like we were at this turning point because of me shutting down after the loss of Noah. For all I know, this other woman came into the picture during that brief, dark cloud in our relationship."

"Okay, I suppose I can say there were times when Ol' Pat didn't come off too bad, but you know good and darn well that insecurity piece was always lingering in the background. Can we agree on that?"

I had to think on that because, to me, Patrick never came across as someone who was jealous or controlling until after I confronted him about that hair accessory being in our home. To me, that was his way of deflecting his guilt onto me and not taking ownership of his actions.

"Vance, no need to even reflect on what he was and was not doing before today. All I care about is today and moving forward."

He grunted. "Yeah, okay, but I still say you're letting him off easy, you never made him answer for having another woman in your home. He knew good and well he was the only one ever in that garage; you should've told him saying I don't know won't cut it." He shook his head. "All you've ever done is love him, and put up with his constant accusations of infidelity. You shouldn't leave this relationship without letting him know how you feel and why you're done. If you take the passive route, he'll try to weasel his way back in."

"Yeah, I hear you. But honestly, the only thing I have to go on is that ponytail holder and my gut. The stronger of the two was my woman's intuition, which was telling me something wasn't right."

I never thought Patrick's insecurities were warranted. After our son passed on, I disconnected emotionally, and as my healing began, he couldn't shake the feeling that someone else was the cause for my transition from depression to happiness. There wasn't a day that went by that I didn't have to defend my actions and profess my love. I was tired of having to calm his nerves. It wasn't like it did much good, and the more insecure he got, the wilder his actions became.

When Patrick came to my job and attacked my boss, I realized things were really getting out of control and I no longer wanted to be in a relationship where this was okay. I could recall the conversation we had after that day and Patrick was so blinded by his rage and could not, or would not, see the error of his ways. As far as he was concerned, our relationship was spiraling because I was the one stepping out.

"Why are you doing this, Patrick?" I pleaded, following him out to the garage.

He stopped short, causing us to run into each other. "I'm not the one gallivanting around town, looking for a new love. I'm not losing you to some dude from work. What's his name?"

"Winston is my coworker. I've told you that so many times."

"A coworker that has to call you all times of the day? Does he know you have a husband?"

I held up my hand. "I'm representing you. I'm wearing your ring, your name, and I surround myself with evidence of our love on a daily basis. Are you even serious right now?"

"If you love me so much, you'll quit that job."

I almost did just that – quit my job. That is, until I found that hair tie with the blonde hair lying in the garage. I kept that evidence in a Ziploc bag. It'd been hidden in my jewelry box for the past six months. I don't know why I kept it. Not like I pushed the issue once he said he didn't know where it came from.

That stupid garage. He claimed it as his. That and the woodshed in the backyard. His man caves. I walked toward the garage and opened the door, looking around at his lair of wall-to-wall gardening tools. Funny how that wasn't the only hoe he enjoyed using. He took good care of his things. He had a level of OCD that surprised me when I found proof of his affair.

I stared down at his toolbox. That monstrosity. It was black as tar, and the length and width of a picnic table. I never understood why he needed to have one that size. I lifted the lid and glanced over his tools. There were hardly enough tools inside to even fill it up. I started to pull on the drawers, but they appeared to be jammed. Overstuffed, I was sure.

I tugged a little harder and stumbled backward. The drawer flung open, slinging tools and DVDs across the floor.

"*Shoot*. That's what I get for being nosey," I murmured. "But no use stopping what I started."

I grabbed a stack of the DVDs from the floor. Each was labeled, but I couldn't make out what they were.

"10-6.10.15. 9-5.1.10…what the heck is this?" I turned them over in my hand and started toward the living room. I got in front of the television and cursed when I recalled that I'd packed up the DVD player. It made sense to give it to him. He tended to watch more movies than I did. I was more likely to stream or watch films or shows on Hulu or Netflix.

I went over to the desk to use the DVD player on my laptop. "Okay, let's see what we got here."

As the video loaded, I squinted and grimaced at the sight of a man sitting in a lounge chair. He appeared to be at a pool party.

"Probably the pool party where he met blondie," I say under my breath.

I find peace in knowing this footage wasn't recorded in our home, but I don't turn away yet because I'm waiting for my husband to make his cameo. I don't know why I want to see him on this film, I guess doing so will give me peace of mind in knowing I was doing the right thing in asking my husband to leave.

The gentleman began to smile and reclined his chair when a young woman appeared before him. As the seconds ticked, my heart began to race as I took in the scene. The young woman couldn't have been any more than twelve or thirteen years old. Maybe younger. My eyes teared up as reality began to sink in.

"*Sweet* Jesus!" I yelled out as the man's intentions became clear. My stomach clenched. I released everything I had in me on the living room floor.

CHAPTER EIGHT

BRITTAIN

PREPPING FOR MY MORNING RUN, I extended my legs and stretched my arms over my head. I rolled my shoulders back and then my neck in a circle. I was pumped to get out there. I put on my black and neon green sneakers, matching tights, and tank top. The bright colors mirrored my mood, and it didn't hurt that the colors looked amazing against my complexion. I pulled my locks into a high ponytail before bending down to stretch my back.

I looked out across the field and took in the lush, green grass at the park. What I loved most about our route was catching sight of the beautiful, Earth Goddess, floral sculpture at the Atlanta Botanical Gardens. That art screamed girl power each time I passed it. Everyone in the group laughed at me when I mentioned it, but for whatever reason, seeing it pushed me that extra mile. The sun was beginning to peek out from behind the clouds when I saw my girl, Wanda approaching. I knew it was time to get moving.

"Good morning, Sis. You ready to get these miles in?" Wanda asked. She was the first person I met when I joined the running group. She had on a bright yellow and gray mesh top with gray compression leggings. I guess she was in a peppy mood as well.

"You know it. Especially before this rain kicks in." I looked up at the dark clouds that approached in the distance.

She sucked her teeth. "Here we go. You won't melt. Trust me."

I scrunched up my nose and pushed her shoulder. "Anyway, let's go, hater."

We started on our run. I couldn't wait to sweat Kenneth out of my head. He'd been calling, texting, Facebook messaging, and driving by, trying to see me every day. I hadn't gotten the house key back from him yet, but he knew better than to come over again.

I was so lost in my thoughts, I didn't realize more members of our group had caught up with us.

"Hey, ladies. Let's get it."

"Whoop-whoop," they cheered.

My endorphins were high and I was moving at a great pace with some ol' school Lil Jon in my ear. I looked around at my group and we were all getting it in. It was a great workout, or it *was*, until I noticed a new, unwelcomed jogger out the corner of my eye. Kenneth's wife.

That was motivation to run a little bit harder, but I'll be darned if the heifer couldn't run, too.

"Excuse me, Brittain! Brittain!" I could hear her huffing and puffing, hot on my tail. "I know you hear me calling you."

I didn't look back. I ran all the way up the hill, past the upscale port-o-potty, and over the bridge to the parking deck. I whipped the keys from my tiny front pocket in my tights, pressed the keyless ignition on my key fob, and started my car. As soon as I got to it, I jumped in my Jeep Grand Cherokee and sped home. These two were not gonna give me any peace.

Thirty minutes later, I was back in front of my townhouse in Vinings. I pulled into the garage, shut the engine off, and sat parked with my eyes closed. How in the world did I get here? When I met Kenneth, I wasn't even seeking a man at all. I was at

Wednesday WindDown at Centennial Park, listening to live music with some friends, when Kenneth came and stood next to my chair. He had on a suit and tie. I figured he must work in the area and had walked over. I recalled that day and had been thinking about it every day since I found out he was married.

"Do you know who this is performing?" he asked.

"It's a local act called Soul Cartel," I responded, nonchalantly. I'd had a long day at the hospital and wasn't really looking to chat.

"Oh, they're pretty hot," he replied while loosening his tie. "Will you save my spot right here if I buy you a drink?"

My brow raised and my curiosity piqued. I took the line and bit. "Sure, I'll take a bottle of water."

He smirked. "Someone knows how to party, bet. I'll be right back."

The water returned, but not the man. Instead, there were two teenage girls.

"Excuse me, some guy asked me to bring this to you," one girl said, passing me the water and a business card. I turned the card over and saw he'd written his cell number on the back.

"Kenneth Wallace? Okay, mystery man." I looked around to see if I could spot him anywhere, but just as quickly as he came, he was gone.

I remembered going back and forth on whether to even call him. Boy, I wish I would have followed my first mind and chucked that business card along with the empty water bottle that day.

I got out of the car, grabbed my purse from the trunk and headed inside. I walked into the kitchen and straight to the fridge to get a bottle of water. Running away from Kenneth's wife had really worked up a thirst. I opened the bottle and started to chug it down. Closing the door, I jumped and spilled it all when I saw Kenneth's wife standing there.

I reeled back, clutching my chest as I took a beat to collect myself, then let out an explosion of expletives. My head swirled. How long had she been in here? Had she come by my home when I wasn't around? This was too much.

As Candace stood there, unbothered by my reaction, I gritted my teeth, balled up my fists, and took two steps toward her. "What the hell? How did you get in here?"

She held up the key I had made for Kenneth. "Guess you forgot about this, but I'll leave it here for you." She placed the key on the counter and held her hands up.

"Listen, I know I'm wrong for coming here and just dropping into your world, but we need to talk."

I walked up on her, fire in my eyes. "Nah, hell, the only thing we need to discuss is you leaving." I pushed her toward the front door.

She resisted and stood her ground. "I'm not leaving until you hear me out, and then if this conversation ends the way I hope it will, you won't hear from me again and we can both get what we want."

I paused and took a breath. I guess she was already up in my house, but the minute she tried to break bad, I was gonna clock her.

I crossed my arms and rolled my eyes heavenward. "Fine, get to it."

She inhaled. "Do you mind if I sit?"

"Yup," I retorted.

"Well, may I at *least* have some water?" she pleaded.

"You can have some 'get the hell out my house'."

She threw up her hands. "Okay, okay, I need you to keep seeing Kenneth."

My eyes widened. "Do what now?"

She smirked. I guess she figured she'd regained some power in the conversation. She slid down into a seat at the kitchen table and I couldn't help but to join her. This conversation took a turn I didn't expect.

"What is wrong with you two? I'm not sure if this is a test, but trust and believe, I'm done with your husband."

Though I was in my own home, I started to look around for hidden cameras. I had to be a part of a bad prank or a scripted reality television show.

"I can understand your shock, but once I explain, it will all be clear." She paused. "May I have that water now?"

I rolled my eyes, but rose to get her a bottle from the fridge. The petty in me thought to just get her some water from the tap. I snatched the fridge open and got her a bottle before returning to the table. She took a swallow, her eyes smiling as she replaced the top.

"Thank you. Where was I? *Ah* yes, so Kenneth and I have been happily married for ten years and that's because we left it open, to avoid heartache. Do you follow?"

I shook my head. "Not even a little bit. Just get to the point. Why would you want me to keep seeing your husband?"

She cleared her throat. "If you end things with Kenny, he'll want me to stop seeing *my* boyfriend, Lorenzo."

"*Yeeeah*, it's gonna still be a 'no' for me. Thank you for dropping off the key." I rose from the chair, prompting her to get up as well. I planned to call to have the locks changed just as soon as I pushed her behind out the door.

"He was never supposed to propose to you," she informed me, stopping short in the doorway. "You were just supposed to be what you were—an appetizer—but he always came home for the main course. He and I were in a good place. He messed it up for all of us when he proposed to you. I want him to be happy, and you were a piece of our overall happiness." She adjusted her tote on her wrist. "Truth be told, he's worth more to me dead than alive. Anyway, I hope you'll reconsider."

My eyes bulged. "Worth more dead? Yeah, I can totally feel the love in that statement. You take care."

She shook her head and walked out.

As I closed the door behind her, I locked it, leaning my back against the door. Standing there in the entryway unsettled, I couldn't help but wonder what would make him propose to me. If he knew that was one of the restrictions of their agreement, what would make him risk it all? Maybe he really wanted out and chose me over that farce of a marriage. And if that was the case, would that change the way I felt about him if he did only want me?

CHAPTER NINE

TRISH

AND JUST LIKE THAT, Darren gave up on me without so much as a fight. His inability to argue when he knew I was in the wrong was irksome. I wasn't keeping up mess with my husband for sport. Lately, with all of the changes he'd been going through, I needed to be sure I'd continue to be a part of his transition. Sure my methods could be unorthodox and create unnecessary strains, but I had to push him to draw out his emotions. We'd been married for three years now, and he still didn't realize I pushed his buttons on purpose because I wanted him to react.

Growing up, whenever my parents had a disagreement, they battled it out, but it always led to enlightenment and lovemaking. I wanted Darren to be like my father and scoop me up in his arms. Yes, I know that may have come across as the caveman approach, but every now and then, I needed that from my man. I wanted him to be just as spontaneous in our relationship as he was with switching up his career.

Darren had always dreamed of working in physical therapy, but after getting a summer job as a file clerk in a human resources department, he ended up working his way up from clerk to assistant, and from an assistant to a manager. When he finally made it to director level, all of a sudden, he felt unfulfilled and wanted to get back to his desire to work in physical therapy, which he hadn't mentioned to me in years. If he could flip it and reverse it on his career, who's to say that he wouldn't just up and leave me all of a sudden.

I guess you might say my fear was the real reason I turned to Zach. He wooed me, and made me feel desired. In the beginning, it was meaningless flirtation. But one late night in the office and a nightcap turned into a long, hot and steamy night of sex and remorse. Or at least I felt bad the first time. But the more time Darren spent being a goal chaser, I was plunging deeper into a cat-and-mouse game where I loved being caught. I knew that made me sound horrible, and no one would probably believe me when I said I loved my husband, but I really did love Darren.

I didn't want to be in this dangerous place of no return in our marriage, but here we were. I was caught between hating myself and loving how good it felt to be with someone who paid me some attention. Sure, Darren had tried to do romantic things … now, but it was a little too late. While he was focused on figure out what he wanted for his career, Zach was making me feel wanted. He was a man of action, and Darren waited until I pushed him away to care.

It was never supposed to be this way. I honestly felt bad about blowing up Darren's world the way I did, but after several attempts to make Darren show his love for me, I wouldn't allow myself to feel bad about my feelings for Zach. He was the one I wanted to be with; or at least it seemed to make the most sense to be with him.

Zach could provide the type of life I was accustomed to and he could actually afford a work-life balance to enjoy the fruits of his labor. Darren was on the clock, day in and day out to help provide for us, or at least before his salary took a nosedive and put all of the financial burdens on me. He didn't even bother to consult me before deciding to up and change his life. He just dropped it in my lap, and I had to pretend to be fine with it, be the supportive wife. I should've had a chance to provide input before he moved forward with his plan.

If it sounded like I was upset with him, I wasn't – I was jealous and fearful of what was to come. He wasn't afraid to take a chance and find the job he loved, and me, well I'd been in the same profession for seven years and hadn't even thought of a plan to make parole.

I was thirty years old, and I'd yet to figure out what I was good at and what made me happy. All I had was Darren, and he was out there living life and trying new things. I was bitter and poor Darren had become the outlet for my anger. I didn't feel like I had anything to offer the world, until Zach came along and showed me I had something to be desired. I had sex appeal and he valued it, and made me feel special. He was the only risk in life I'd ever allowed myself to dive into head first without hesitation.

It was last year when Zach pulled me into the unisex stall during the Christmas party. The first time we got together, I felt a tone of remorse. I never imagined I'd be intimate with anyone but my husband this time around; however, I swear that was the most alive I had felt in a long time. I knew once he locked the door, our work relationship would change from harmless flirting to on and off-the-clock secret lovers. Not that it was much of a secret.

There was a lot of buzz around the office, which is one reason I never wanted Darren to come by without letting me know. I wanted to keep him safe from the truth, but today I dropped the reality of our situation on his lap and hoped he'd make it all end. I never expected he'd allow me to walk out the door. I stood outside of the door for a few minutes, expecting him to come after me, but he never came and my heart sank. I guess I had finally pushed him too far and I'm sure seeing me in the car with Zach was more than he could bare. It was over.

I pulled into the parking deck of the high-rise condo Zach and I shared in Hilton Head. When I relocated to South Carolina from Georgia, this area, known for its shopping and golf resorts, was high on my list of places to live. If it wasn't for my relationship with Zach, I don't know if I would have ever made it to this level of luxury on my own, and definitely not with the money or lack thereof, that Darren and I made. Living here with Zach could provide me with a life more comparable to what I was use to when living with my parents. They always made sure I had the best of everything.

I rounded the levels of the parking garage until I got to the fifth floor where Zach and I typically parked our cars. Today, though, I was a little perplexed because there was someone in my space. I went back down to the first floor and found a visitor space. While on five, I took a picture of the license plate of the car in my space so I could report it to security.

My first priority, however, was to go in and relax with a glass of wine. Today's events with Darren had worn me out. I hadn't let Zach know I would be here. I thought it best to let him enjoy his wife one last night before I told him what I expected moving forward. I had been patient and now it was time for me to get my due. I should be Mrs. Zachary Hollister, and I was determined to make that transition.

Using my access card, I walked down the hall toward 503. Zach specifically asked for that number because we met on May 3rd. He was romantic like that, and since Zach was wealthy, he was able to ensure that even if someone was in that space at the time, it would be vacant for us to claim.

"Hi, Trish. How's it going?" my neighbor, Mrs. Forrester, inquired. She was a sweet older lady, but she was super nosey. With Zach and I creeping, the last thing I needed was for her to want to impart wisdom or be all up in our business. I usually tried to avoid her in the halls, but considering I was moving here permanently, I guess I needed to make nice.

I put my key in the door, just in case I needed a quick escape. "Hello, Mrs. Forrester. Everything is going well. How are you?"

She shifted her dentures around. My cue to run. I placed my hand on the doorknob, hoping she'd catch the hint that this wasn't meant to be a conversation, but a brief chat.

"Well, honey," she started, shifting her weight against the wobbly cane, barely holding her upright. Too late for me to run now. "My sciatica has really been bothering me. Just can't seem to get no kind of relief." She began to rub her lower back. "Would you like to come inside for some tea so we can talk some more, dear?"

I plastered a fake smile on my face. The only thing I would love to do was help her find a new wig. That faded gray or purple, matted mess on her head had to have retired long before she did. Talk about a rehired retiree – that wig had seen better days.

"Oh no, but thanks for the offer," I said, patting her on the hand. "Well, I guess I'll see you later."

I hurried and pushed the door open, then closed it behind me. I smiled inwardly as I surveyed my new permanent residence. I walked over to the kitchen area to see what was in the refrigerator. I spotted some veggies and pulled out a skirt steak from the freezer. I would allow the meat to thaw out so I could cook tonight. Or maybe I would order in. Not like Zach would be over tonight. He still had to play pretend with his wife until we came up with his exit strategy.

I put the steak back in the freezer and walked over to the drawer where we kept the take-out menus when I heard what I knew to be the heels of a woman clicking across the floor.

"I'm sorry. Are you lost?" the voice questioned.

I turned around to see a pair of firm legs, hips, and thighs, with a silk robe left open, showing off her toned abs, perky breasts, and a dainty four-leaf clover tattoo on her hip. My mouth hung open as I stared at the nude woman standing comfortably in the living room as if she belonged here. My eyelids fluttered, and I wiped at them, certain I was seeing a mirage. I looked around to make sure I indeed was not lost.

"Uh no, I live here. This is Zach's and *my* condo. We've lived here for years now," I lie. Zach had this place for a while, but of course my official residency here would only be starting today. That wasn't her business. "Did someone let you in?" I eyed her again, not wanting to let my suspicions win. This couldn't be happening.

"Ah, you must be Tuesday and Wednesday. As you can see, I'm Zach's Monday and his Thursday, and well, at times even his Saturday and Sunday." She shimmied and began to giggle before walking over to the living room and plopping down on the sofa.

"How long have you been seeing Zach?" I kept my tone calm, but on the inside, I was blazing hot.

"About three months now. What about you? I'm Chelsey, by the way."

I couldn't stop staring at her. I never figured he would be into redheads. His wife was a blonde, but I guess considering that I'm a black woman, maybe he enjoyed a variety. With the exception of Chelsey's younger physique, we had similar frames. Mine was just the older model.

"Trish," I replied, walking closer to her. I ignored her other question. I was the only one who should be concerned about who he was seeing and for how long. "So…" I seethed. "Where is Zach?"

What on earth did he see in her? I was sure she was in her early twenties, but her behavior was that of a fifth grader transitioning to middle school. The way she constantly fidgeted with her hair and the way she moved like a child overloaded on sweets.

It had to be sex. I couldn't see them having an intelligent conversation.

"He made a coffee run. He should be back soon. I have class in a bit, so he was making sure I had some caffeine for the road. I just haven't gotten dressed yet because, well you know Zachy's appetite." She did the annoying giggle again. "You can hang with me until he gets back, though."

Just as I was about to sit down on the sofa, I saw the tangled sheets thrown across the floor and decided to have a seat at the bar instead. Then again, she was young and this might have been used in a sex act as well.

"You know what, Chesca, I think I'll just come back later."

"Cool and its Chelsey," she offered cheerfully, clearly not catching my condescending tone. "Should I let Zachy know you stopped by?"

"No, I'll let him know. Thank you, Chesca," I said, my voice laced with venom.

Letting myself out, I leaned against the door with my eyes closed only to open them to see Mrs. Forrester standing there in the entryway to her place.

"I guess you met Chelsey, huh?" she asked with a glint in her eyes. "Perhaps, you'd like that tea now?"

I smirked. *Touché, Mrs. Forrester.* "Absolutely, and don't stop pouring until I've gotten the last drop."

She winked and stepped back to let me inside.

CHAPTER TEN

HEIDI

MY HANDS SHOOK. I had been with this man for more than a decade – might as well say I'd been with him for forever. How could this be happening under my own roof? That led to the question of where had this been filmed.

My eyes shot from left to right, scanning the house. My palms started to sweat. I stood to my feet, but my legs wouldn't hold me. Again, I regurgitated.

Wiping my mouth with the back of my hand, I closed my eyes tight, willing away what my eyes saw. What kind of man does this? *A monster*.

My phone rang, jostling me to attention. My vision was blurred as I scanned the room to locate it.

I stumbled toward the living room and retrieved my phone from the couch.

"Hey, Vance, uh puh-puh-lease hurry and come over. I-I'll explain when you get here."

I dropped down onto the sofa, folding my legs beneath me and hugged myself. My new normal was starting out as anything but that, as my mind raced, wondering what other lies were hidden in this house.

My eyes landed on the coffee table where the DVDs lay stacked. Layers of filth, as far as I was concerned. I shook my head. It was a dark thought, but I couldn't help but be grateful we didn't have any more children. I don't know if Patrick would've protected them as a father should, or if he would've tried to sell their innocence to the highest bidder. I closed my eyes, leaning my head against the headrest. I could feel a headache coming on.

What else had he been hiding? I shot up from the chair. The woodshed. I wasn't sure if I had enough energy left in me to tackle any more surprises. But I had to know. I couldn't go a second more knowing I was living in a lie.

Gathering my courage, I went into the kitchen to locate the key. I pulled one drawer after the other…nothing. "The garage," I exclaimed.

I walked through the door and went back to the purveyor of truth. The toolbox. Combing through the place where I found the DVDs, there were receipts, hotel key cards, and photos of young girls.

"You sick bastard," I mumbled. Now, more determined to find the key, I dumped the contents of the box and the key went flying across the room. I shuffled across the room, snatched the key up, and hurried toward the backyard. I stepped on to the plush green grass. His pride and joy. Kentucky Bluegrass. That's what the neighbors had and he was hard pressed that we would have it, too.

"What a façade." I huffed, shaking my head. I swallowed hard as I slid the key into the lock. I really didn't want it to work. Didn't want to see what was behind these doors. But deep down, I knew I'd never have peace if I didn't know everything there was to know. Pulling the doors apart, I shut my eyes tight.

"You can do this, Heidi. Get it over with." Opening my eyes, I looked around and was relieved to see nothing out of the norm.

The shed was full of shadows from the small slits where sun managed to sneak into the room. I'd never really walked into the shed. This was Patrick's place. I felt around for a switch and flipped it up once my hand found it.

With my vision no longer restricted by darkness, I looked around the room and once again, I felt a sense of relief. There were just old boxes filled with family photos, two kennels from when we had twin terriers, and parts from unfinished projects Patrick promised to do around the house. Other than a few gardening tools and his riding lawn mower, there was nothing out of the ordinary to be found.

While none of this changed my thoughts on Patrick and the filthy DVDs, I was glad there was nothing more. I couldn't take any more surprises.

Satisfied with my snooping, I turned to walk back out.

"Please, don't leave," a voice whispered.

"Shut up. You'll get us killed," another whined.

I froze in place. Surely, I'd lost my mind. "Hello? Who's there?"

"Shhh, they'll hurt us," another voice called.

I turned, my hand flying to my mouth. What had Patrick done? "I won't hurt you. I'm Heidi. Please, come out so I can get you help."

Turning left and right, I didn't see any signs of life in the room other than my own.

"Stop talking to us and go. She'll hurt our family. Please, just go."

She? Who were they talking about? Perhaps, there was another woman after all and she had gotten him involved in this mess. What the heck was going on?

"I'll protect you from whoever she might be. Please, let me help you."

A beat and then, "Back here. In the kennel."

Hand over my mouth, I stifled a scream. Wailing was not going to help get these two to safety.

I bent down. My palms were wet, slipping the creaky handle from my grip. The crate creaked opened as I slid the latch from the holster. Reaching my hand inside, I inhaled and braced myself as a tiny hand squeezed mine.

I took in the sight of a petite, blonde haired, blue-eyed adolescent. Her hair was matted and stringy, lifeless and faded. The bags under her eyes let me know she couldn't have been sleeping. It was all coming together—the hair tie and the secrecy. Patrick was in deep, it would seem. Child pornography, kidnapping, and Lord knows what else he'd gotten involved in.

"I'm going to get you out of here, girls. Once we get inside the house, we'll call the police. Everything will be okay."

They nodded their heads, but the vacant look in their eyes indicated they didn't expect a miracle. Truth is, I wasn't sure if we'd make it out of this alive myself.

CHAPTER ELEVEN

DARREN

I GRABBED a beer from the refrigerator and retreated to the den off the side of the kitchen. This was supposed to be my man cave, but Trish had taken it over to store more of her shoes. Since she decided to leave me and all her things, I put her excess shoe collection in a garbage bag and lugged it into the garage. Of course the closet in the master bedroom still stored several of her clothes and the remainder of her shoes, but now I had at least one room I could now go in and not have to think about her. I smiled to myself. This was the most at peace I'd felt in a long time.

I'd allowed her to emasculate me. Telling me how to dress, criticizing me in the bedroom, letting me know on several occasions that she was the breadwinner. It was for the best that she'd left. Now she could be who she thought she was with that pompous boss of hers.

"Hey, Ren. I finished warming everything up. Sorry it wasn't fresh out the grease, had I know earlier that you would be inviting me over today, I could've planned ahead."

"I'm not complaining at all. I just appreciate you doing this," I say.

"The pleasure is mine, but next time let me know. I could've brought a change of clothes and just freshened up here."

I eyed Veronica, taking in her long legs, full hips, and pouty lips. Her dark black hair highlighted her light brown eyes against her coffee complexion. The girl was gorgeous.

"I was surprised you asked me over. What made you finally take me up on my offer?"

"I just didn't want to eat alone and figured it would be a good time to get to know one another."

Veronica worked in the deli at the grocery store across from my job. I often went in to get lunch, and every time I ate there, Veronica asked me why my wife wasn't making my lunch.

"Big strong fella like you, I know you need more than a chicken salad sandwich."

"Must you give me a hard time every day I come in? I happen to enjoy it."

"Yeah. Well, I think you'd like my Chicken Marsala better. As a matter-uh-fact," she whispered, looking around, *"why don't you come by tonight and taste it?"*

She scribbled her name and number down on a recipe card and slid it to me.

I extended my hand across the counter, pushing the indecent proposal back toward her. "Happily married, but flattered."

Walking away from her that day, I was proud of myself. I respected the sanctity of my marriage and upheld my promise, only to find out my loving wife was getting what she needed elsewhere. No need to resist Veronica any longer. Trish had made her choice. There was no reason I should get dusty waiting to be recalled from the shelf. As luck would have it, I called in a to-go order, and Veronica answered. An hour later, she arrived at my door with a meal and a warm smile.

"Uh, hello," she beckoned, bringing me back to the present. "I asked if we were eating in the kitchen or in the den?"

"Let's get one thing straight. It's a man cave," I said, giving us both a light laugh. "So why don't we eat in the kitchen? I want to give you my undivided attention and if we stay in here, I'll be watching some kind of sport."

She nodded. "The kitchen it is, then. This is a really nice home, Darren. So, um, how much time do we have before the wrecking ball and chain comes home? It would be wild if she caught us in the act."

I eyed her with suspicion, wondering why she'd chosen me that day in the store. She knew I was married, but flirted without restriction. Perhaps she wouldn't want me anymore if she knew I was separated.

"Why are you worried about my wife? She won't be catching us doing anything other than eating, right?"

I planted the question to get her reaction and I wasn't happy with what I got.

She squealed. "Oh, come on, don't you think it would be hot? Just think about it. She comes up the steps from a long day and sees me on your bed with my legs touching the ceiling. If anything—if she's like me—shoot, I'd be turned on."

As she stuck out her tongue and rolled her body in a circle, I frowned and shook my head. I wanted to protest that she wasn't like her, but considering the way Trish was *enjoying* her boss in the parking lot, I don't know what she would do anymore.

"Veronica, I didn't invite you over to talk about my wife. Let's just enjoy dinner," I spat. "Please understand, while I do find you to be a very attractive woman, the only thing I want tonight is good conversation. Maybe down the line, it could be more, but that's not what I want from you right now. If you expected more than that, then you should probably be out."

In all truth, Veronica was not really my type for a long-term relationship and I didn't want to make her a good-time girl that could turn into a problem I couldn't easily get rid of if things went left. I had enough problems already with figuring out what to do about Trish. Sexing the girl from the deli would have to wait.

She pouted. "I had you pegged all wrong. You're a bore, Darren. You've got all of this in front of you," she said, squeezing her DD cups together. "You're going to pass on this? Wow, I don't know if I'm more disappointed or annoyed that I wasted my time."

I nodded. "You know what, that makes the both of us. Why don't I pack you a to-go plate? I'm sure it's safe to say this date is over."

She threw up her hands. "Fine by me. Don't bother with the plate. I have someone else lined up for an hour from now. I always make sure to have a backup plan."

"Per-*fect*. You can let yourself out. I'm sure you recall how you slithered in."

She rose from the chair and stormed out, slamming the door behind her.

I ran my hand across my bald head. It was a good thing I didn't have any hair. Trish would've caused it all to fall out with the stress she was putting me through.

I chuckled. Even after all of this, Trish had my heart and she was the only one I would want to go through all this hell with. I wasn't sure if our marriage was salvageable, but I knew I loved her.

Walking over to the living room, I sat at our shared desk and logged in to track Trish's phone. She constantly pushed me, and it was time I responded and stopped being passive. It was time Zach, Trish, and I had a conversation. I know some people would say I'm weak to take my wife back after all I'd seen and the things she said to me, but I made vows and I believe I had to at least try to figure out if there was still hope of us. I was going to save my marriage, no matter what it took. I wanted her to know I wasn't giving up on her.

CHAPTER TWELVE

BRITTAIN

I FIDDLED with my locks as I waited for Kenneth to arrive. I knew it was idiotic to want to hear him out, but I was curious. After speaking to his wife, it was all that I could think about. It was half past three, and I was becoming more anxious by the minute. Kenneth was supposed to have arrived thirty minutes and two drinks ago. Yet here I was, sitting here feeling duped again.

"Would you like an appetizer while you wait?" the bartender inquired for the second time since I arrived.

I shook my head. I was sitting at the rooftop bar at Six Feet Under and had been waiting for thirty minutes now, enjoying Atlanta's skyline. This was one of the many restaurants where Kenneth and I shared a moment. We planted seeds here. The staff knew us by name and greeted us with hugs each time we dined here. Now this place would be merely a memory in the rearview mirror of our relationship.

"Is this seat taken?" a baritone voice inquired.

I turned to stare into a pair of deep sunken, chocolate eyes, and felt at home in them. There was something about him that felt familiar. His pearly white smile, mahogany complexion, and bushy brows around his offset eyes all teased my memory bank—

I knew him from somewhere. His smooth head was clean shaven, the only hair being the salt and pepper beard on his face which gave him a look of distinction.

I smiled. "No, it appears that seat is vacant. Have at it."

I adjusted the strap on my peach sundress that seemed to slide off my shoulder every two seconds, and moved my purse to the hook under the bar area to make room for the sexy stranger.

"Thank you, Miss." I watched as he waved at the bartender.

His buttoned-up attire all the way down to the Stacey Adams dress shoes made me wonder if he was here on business, or perhaps he worked for the state or the city of Atlanta. I checked his hand and didn't see a wedding ring, though that meant nothing now, considering Kenneth hadn't been wearing one when I met him either.

"Let me get a Coke," he ordered, before turning his attention to the news on the television mounted behind the bar.

I looked back at the entrance of the restaurant one last time before giving up on Kenneth. I took comfort in knowing he wouldn't be waiting on my sofa tonight since I'd changed the locks. I could officially move on with my life. I sipped on my cocktail and examined the man next to me as the bartender sat his drink down. "Excuse me, but do I know you? I can't place you, but I feel like I know your face from somewhere."

He took a sip from his glass and chuckled. "Dang, that forgettable, huh?"

I squinted my eyes and smiled. "I'm sorry. Don't say that. I recognize you, but I can't seem to figure out where we've met."

"Elias Sanders. I used to sit behind you in—"

"Mrs. Shelnutt's class. Oh my gosh, North Cobb High School. Wow, throwback indeed," I exclaimed. "Well, I must say you look great."

He rubbed his chin. "Well, thank you. Too bad you didn't think much of me then."

I threw my head back in laughter. "Wait a minute. If you were *that* into me, you could've spoke."

He guffawed. "Yeah, right. Me, the band nerd, tryin' to holla at one of the popular girls. Nah. I was ridiculed enough during high school."

I shook my head. "Oh please. Who was gonna mess with you? And anyway, I wasn't *that* popular and I spoke to everyone. You should've tried me out back in the day." I took a sip of my drink, eyeing him over the rim. "I might have said yes."

His head bobbed as he leaned in closer to me. "And what about present day? Are you seeing anyone now?"

I looked at my naked ring finger and out toward the skyline before returning my gaze to him. "It appears that I'm wide open to something new."

He held up his glass and I clinked mine against it in celebration of what could be. Kenneth did me a favor not showing up. I needed to move on. There was nothing left to know. He had an affair and I had fraud. No need to recycle hearts made of glass. We were broken, and there wasn't enough glue to make me mend that mess.

PULLING INTO THE GARAGE, I smiled to myself. My day had taken an unexpected turn for the better. Running into a former classmate had been refreshing. The fact that he was handsome didn't hurt the situation either.

Walking into the house, I strolled over to the living room and grabbed my yearbook from the bookshelf. I flipped through the pages and allowed myself to reminisce. I did participate in several clubs—yearbook, pep squad, a cheerleader, and majorette—I guess I was a part of the *cool* crowd.

As if on cue, my phone beeped.

Elias: Had a good time. Next time we can meet on purpose. TTYL.

Me: Sounds good to me...bring your saxophone.

Elias: Never leave home without it. Impromptu dinner and a mini concert?

Me: Hmmm, eight o'clock, my place?

Elias: Music to my ears. See you soon.

I texted him my address. The young me didn't appreciate guys in the band, but I could always use some good sax in my life now. That was my favorite instrument. I smiled. I hadn't stopped smiling since I left the restaurant, to be honest. I didn't want our time together to end, but Elias got a call and had to get back to work. We were so busy flirting and reminiscing, we didn't even get around to what we were doing in the now. Guess I would find out tonight.

I surprised myself taking him up on his offer. I preferred to have more time to prep and plan, but I had already lost so much time dealing with Kenneth. This was a much-appreciated change of pace for me. I had a few hours before he'd arrive, so I had some time to get it together or at least find a take-out menu.

I looked in the refrigerator. I had forgotten I'd pulled out some ground turkey this morning so I could make spaghetti tonight. Pasta, garlic bread, and salad would be a quick and easy dinner to prepare, and I would have more than enough time to spruce up the place and freshen up for my date.

Before I got started, I plopped down on the sofa to catch the evening news. I typically watched the evening news with a glass of Merlot, but I already had a nice buzz from earlier to prepare me for the anticipated nightly drama.

"Police are investigating what appears to be a homicide. Local residents were stunned at the commotion heard in this Peachtree Hills home earlier today. Thirty-eight year-old Kenneth Wallace was pronounced dead on arrival at Grady Memorial

Hospital. Wallace was stabbed multiple times. His wife, Candace Wallace, is the prime suspect. More to come tonight at ten."

My ears replayed the names over and over again. I couldn't un-hear it. This explained why Kenneth couldn't meet me. He was dead. My hand flew to my mouth as Candace's words replayed in my head. *"He's worth more to me dead than alive."*

CHAPTER THIRTEEN

HEIDI

THE GIRLS COULD BARELY WALK, let alone run to the house. Their legs were weak. Lord knows how long they had been scrunched in that small space or how long they had been held here living in fear. I could only think the little bit of strength they had mustered up to move was in their hope of getting out of here alive, or maybe they were motivated from fear of being caught outside. Both of the girls had matted hair, their faces covered in smut, and their clothes reeked of urine.

Once again, I resisted the urge to cry as I shook off the images I saw in the video earlier. These poor girls. I shuddered imagining the horrific things they had seen at their young age at the hands of these perverts. The tattered and worn, oversized t-shirts and khaki bottoms looked as if they were never given a change of clothing. I wanted to feed them, let them get a bath, and allow them to put on some fresh clothes, but I knew the best thing for me to do was to just get them away from here.

"Uh, so we're going to go inside and then I'll grab my phone and keys. We'll go to the police and they can help us find your families. How's that sound?" I said. My eyes were darting from left to right, canvassing the house for a weapon. Just in case.

"Please, just hurry. They will kill us," the oldest of the two whimpered.

"I promise I'll do my best to protect you both. What are your names?"

"I'm Ana and she's Willa."

"Can we have some water please?" Willa, the younger of the two asked.

"Sure, sure, um, come on. I'll get two waters and then we'll get going."

My hands shook as I grabbed the refrigerator door. But my heart dropped as I heard the sound of a car pulling up outside. My eyes shot across the kitchen toward the living room and back to the two young lives I knew I had to protect. I peeked through the blinds and swallowed hard, noticing it was Patrick's car.

"Okay, girls. I want you both to go up to my bedroom and hide in the closet. It's the room at the top right."

"Please, don't leave us alone," Willa said, as she held on to my arm.

"Sweetie," I said, taking a breath, "we don't have time. Please go upstairs and be as quiet as you can, okay?"

Ana nodded her head in understanding, grabbing Willa and dragging her up the stairs. I sprang to action and hurried to the living room. I had changed the locks, so Patrick wouldn't be able to get in without my answering the door.

I grabbed the DVDs, stuffed them under the sofa cushion and took a calming breath as I walked over to open the front door. I scowled at Patrick as soon as our eyes connected.

"You shouldn't just come over unannounced. What do you want?"

"I still live here, too," he said, in a steely tone. "You can't keep me from coming inside the house where I pay bills."

I clenched my teeth. "I will ask you again. Why are you here and what do you want?"

Shuffling his keys in his hands, he diverted his eyes away from me. He held his hands up in defense. "I'm not here to argue. Just trying to get some things and then I'm out."

He walked around me to head upstairs. I shuffled back in front of him, blocking him from taking another step.

I shook my head. "You can make a list of what you need and I'll get it to you. There's no need for you to go up there just to grab clothes. I can get those for you."

He raised his chin. "You got somebody up there, don't you?"

"I'm so sick of you. You're the one having an affair. There's not a car in the driveway except yours." I dropped my head and took a beat. "I've had a long day. Please, just go. I can schedule a time for you to come get your things tomorrow. I'm just not ready for this today. It's all just too much."

I had to get him out of here. I didn't trust that those two little girls would keep their cool much longer, knowing he was down here. I had to think of their safety.

"Listen, Heidi, I'm sorry, okay," he mumbled. "It's not what you think. Me and Coryn…that's Suzanne's roommate. I mean, she's into me, but it's not like that."

Sweat beads formed around the nape of my neck and my mouth felt chalky. "I don't know what or who Coryn is, nor do I care," I choked out. "Please, just grab your crap over there in that box and go."

He looked at the box in the corner of the room and back at me with anger in his eyes. He was no longer attempting to take the nice guy approach.

"Why are you being so hasty? The only logical explanation behind you rushing me out the door is that you're hiding something or someone," he accused, looking back up the stairs. "I know our relationship has hit a rough patch, but you're trying to place all of the blame on me and it isn't fair, Heidi." His lips formed a straight line and his eyes narrowed. "I won't allow you to make me look foolish, gallivanting around with some…ugh, what is that smell?" he asked, walking toward the desk.

My eyes grew wide as I remembered I'd left the laptop open. "No, no, wait, I got sick. Don't go over there."

I ran across the room, trying to keep the situation from taking yet another ugly turn, but it was too late.

"Where did you get this?" he asked, his voice filled with worry, holding up the CD holder.

"*That's what you care about?* Where I got it doesn't matter, Patrick. You're sick, sick, sick."

He ran his hand over his salt and pepper beard, and took a sharp breath. "Calm down. It's not what it looks like." Taking a breath, he approached the subject again. "Let me just explain. I'll tell you everything."

I shuddered as the pressure of what I knew to be the barrel of a gun pressed against the back of my neck.

"You don't need to explain anything to her. It's exactly what it looks like, *Heidi*. And what of it? She's not going to do anything about it, Patrick," Suzanne said, in a malicious tone. "'Cause if she even flinches an inch, she'll die."

Finding those CDs, I knew Patrick was involved in some mess, but with the two innocent girls in the shed and now to be held at gunpoint by his sister, I was fearful of who else might come knocking on the door if I even made it past these two. I started to send up prayers for the girls' and my safety once all was said and done. They didn't deserve this and I knew they probably had a family out there praying for their safe return. I had to keep my composure. My only option was to comply and hope that my cousin Vance would arrive soon.

I just needed to do what Suzanne said and I would make it out of this okay. I had to believe the girls and I would make it out of this alive. Inhaling deeply, I lifted my hands and kept my eyes on Patrick, careful not to move an inch.

CHAPTER FOURTEEN

TRISH

I CLOSED the door behind me as I walked out of Mrs. Forrester's condo, seething. She and I chatted for a little over an hour, and boy, had she filled me in on the so-called love of my life. Zach really had me open. All this time and I was just another woman. Not the other woman, but just another notch on his belt.

I thought I was special, but according to Mrs. Forrester, he had a new one over every night, and then there was Chelsey who told me herself that she was a regular and had certain days of the week where she was scheduled to appear. As I stood in front of his door, pondering my next move, I thought back on all I'd learned over the past hour.

"I wasn't sure if I was across the hall from a brothel or if he'd opened a hotel over there. I was sure that wasn't the only thing getting opened, if you know what I mean," Mrs. Forrester insinuated as she poured me a cup of tea.

"That many, huh? I guess you think I'm a fool."

She shrugged. "No more than those other gals he got waltzing through there. Listen, honey, you seem like a nice young lady. You should leave him alone. He don't seem right in the head. I think there's more to him than just being a womanizer."

I tilted my head. "How do you mean?"

She leaned in closer. "And you ain't heard none of this from me, but outside of you, I've never seen any of those women as much as I've seen you." She paused, shifting her teeth around before she spoke again. "It's strange really; come to think of it, you're the only one I've seen come and go…with the exception of that Chelsey girl, I don't recollect seeing any of the others leaving after their visit. You're the only one that drives over here, too. He sends a car service for those other gals."

As I stood staring at his front door, I wondered why his dealings with me were different. Maybe I shouldn't have been upset—I was the chosen one. I was special. He didn't mind me driving over and claiming a parking space. He had set me apart from the rest.

I removed my key from my purse and started to let myself in, but considering what I knew now, I thought it might be best to let him make that call. I lifted my hands to knock, just as he was coming out.

I was greeted with expletives, followed by a lukewarm welcome. He pulled the door closed behind him, only leaving a slit open. "Trish, darling. What brings you by? I was just headed out."

"Hey. I just wanted to come by and see you. Sorry to drop by unannounced, but since I'm here, I hoped that we could talk."

My mind raced. He seemed different. Unbeknownst to him, we were different. I was planning to leave my husband to be with him full-time, only now, I was learning he only considered me as an appointment on his weekly list of calendar girls. Just another romp of the week.

"It's always a pleasure to see your lovely face, and if it were any other day, I would love to have you come inside so we could spend some time together. However, now is not a good time. But hey, tomorrow is Tuesday, so I'll see you then, okay?"

I noted the sweat beads along his brow. *Probably from sexing up that wench who was in there earlier,* I thought. I wondered had she left and gone to class already. Based on our earlier encounter, she should've been on her way or in class by now.

"Zach, what's going on? I really need to talk to you, now," I said, pushing past him.

My eyes bulged as I screamed at the sight of her. Blood oozed from the back of Chelsey's head and on to the carpet. Her eyes were open wide staring back into mine. I knew the fear behind them mirrored my own. Her face was barely recognizable, but that tattoo told her story. I closed my eyes as the tears started to fall.

I opened them and turned back towards Zach, trying to figure out my options – though I knew I really had none.

Running his fingers through his hair, Zach cast his eyes downward, taking a deep breath before closing the door. "Trish, I really wish you hadn't done that."

"Zach, don't… I won't tell a soul," I whimpered. "I promise, I won't, just please let me go," I pleaded, walking toward him, which was the only way out.

He shook his head. "I know you won't, because you won't get a chance."

As he lunged at me, I saw flashes of the brief moments I allowed Darren to love me. The day he proposed and the day I accepted, and the day I said I was home sick and he agreed to relocate us to South Carolina. Then when I told him I wanted a home, he made it happen with some land he acquired from his grandfather only for me to throw it all away. Now, as Zach's hands were surrounding my throat and I was kicking and screaming for my life, struggling to get free, I realized I had already had the kind of love and life that I desired after all.

CHAPTER FIFTEEN

BRITTAIN

I COULDN'T BRING myself to get up from the sofa. I knew I should call the police and tell them what I knew, but did I really know anything at all? I mean, a lot of people make slick comments when they're mad at their significant other. Who was I to be Candace's judge and jury? For all I knew, she was just venting.

My talking to the police would no doubt make me a suspect. Everything about my situation with Kenneth made me fit to be questioned. Though I was unknowingly in a love affair, the police would only see me as the other woman. That alone would make them say I had a motive. No, it was better that I mind my business.

A knock at the door took me out of my thoughts. I looked down at my watched and cursed. I can't believe I'd been sitting here for two hours and accomplished nothing I planned to do before his arrival. After seeing Kenneth's story on the news, I flipped to other stations to see if they had any additional information and then I started combing the Internet. I even visited his and Candace's Facebook pages to see what their last status updates were. Needless to say, I hadn't freshened up or prepared the meal I promised to cook.

I opened the door to find Elias there toting a bottle of wine and his saxophone case. There went my fresh start.

I managed a weak smile. "Hey, come on in."

"Whoa, that's not excitement to see me. Should we reschedule?"

I shook by head and took a step back. "No, please come in."

Elias followed me into the living room. I lowered myself down onto the sofa and patted the cushion next to me, requesting that he join me.

"Today has been crazy. When I ran into you at the restaurant this afternoon, I was there waiting for my ex-fiancé, Kenneth at the restaurant. When you showed up, it was exactly what I needed to stop thinking about him. Then I get home to find out the reason he didn't show is because he's dead."

His eyes went big. "Dead?"

I nodded. "Dead. Murdered. Probably by his wife."

He frowned. "You said his name was Kenneth? Is the last name Wallace?"

Now my eyes went big. I nodded. How did he know?

He rubbed his beard. "Dang, that's wild. You know when I got that call at the restaurant and had to leave, it was to report to the scene. I'm a detective with the APD."

My hand flew to my mouth. "Whoa, I can't even process. You had to report to the scene of Kenneth's murder?" He nodded and I just sat, momentarily speechless. "You're a cop and the day you re-enter my life is the day you investigate the murder of my ex? This…is…crazy."

He reached for my hands. "Are you okay?"

"Yeah, I'll be fine. This is just a lot to take in, you know." I shook my head. "I'm so sorry. This wasn't the evening we had in mind."

"Listen, I know you were going to cook, but why don't I see what you got in the fridge and create one of my special, 'this'll do' meals."

A hearty laugh came out of me as I nodded. "I appreciate it. I've thawed some meat out to make spaghetti, so you won't have to stretch your imagination too far."

"Oh, I can work with that. You relax and I'll find my way to the pots and pans." He rose from the seat and crossed the hall to get to the kitchen.

Elias was exactly what I needed to close out the evening. So far, he'd managed to make my day better twice within a few hours.

As Elias found his way to the kitchen, I was just about to go and turn off the news and reset the mood with some light jazz when I heard another knock at the door. This one more thunderous than the last.

I pulled open the door and gasped. I wasn't expecting Candace, Kenneth's crazy wife, to be standing on the other side with blood-splattered clothes and a knife I knew from the news to be the murder weapon.

"Candace!" My breath caught as I searched for what to say next. I gripped the door handle to help steady my legs, which suddenly felt unstable. Common sense was urging me to close the door; too bad the nonsensical side of me was in charge. "Um, I saw the news. I'm sorry about—"

Her eyes wild. She whispered, "I told you to take him. I told you he was no good to me. But *no*, you had to be selfish and couldn't do the right thing for us all."

Eyeing the knife, I raised my hands in defense before I spoke to her. "Candace, listen. Why don't you stay right here and let me call some help for you? Everything is going to be all right, okay?"

I started to push the door closed, but she was stronger than I anticipated, shoving it back open.

"No, no, no, no, you can't just keep leaving. First, you left him in the park. Then you left the opportunity I gave you to keep him safe, but no…that didn't work for what Brittain wanted, did it?" She cackled and stopped abruptly.

Eyeing the knife, I started looking around to see what I could grab to defend myself with if the need came. "Candace, you're not making sense. Kenneth being married changed everything for me. I wouldn't have given him any play if I had known he was married."

She pointed the knife in my direction as she spoke, "So why reach out to him? If you were done, then you wouldn't need to see him again. But that was your plan, right Brittain? What was that about?"

I winced. I guess she wasn't the only one who sounded like a crazy person. "About that… Listen, I'm not sure what I expected to happen. I just—"

"You just what? You wanted him, but just didn't want me to know about it." She waved the knife back and forth in front of my face. "You didn't think Kenny told me that you was gonna meet up with him today? Poor thing was probably worried then about missing out on her man, but it was too late then. You had already made your choice. And now…now you want to help me." She nervously severed her clothing, the knife tearing at her skin as blood seeped through her trousers.

My eyes shifted and I noticed Elias moving toward us out the corner of my eye. With the shock of it all, I had almost forgotten he was in the kitchen. He motioned for me to be quiet, and I attempted to keep her talking.

"Candace, I thought my leaving Kenneth alone was the best thing for everyone. Even after you came by and gave me your blessing, I didn't think it was right for me to continue in that type of relationship. It wasn't what I wanted."

She crouched down, thrusting the knife into the floor. I looked over to Elias, but he was no longer standing there. He had better be getting help. It would be just my luck that he lied about being a cop and was an unarmed file clerk at the precinct. I thought to reach down and grab the knife, but decided against. Based on the way Candace shoved the door back open, she had some crackhead strength I wasn't fit to compete against.

"Our marriage was over. It had been for years," she confessed, rising back up to face me. "We agreed to have an open marriage, but when he proposed to you, it ruined our agreement. I wasn't going to give up my boyfriend for a dull and boring life with Kenneth. When he said he wanted to try to make just us work, I knew what I had to do."

"What did you do?" I asked. I had to hear her say it. I'm sure Elias wanted that confession, too.

With a Cheshire cat grin, she said, "I killed him, of course. It's like I told you. He's worth more to me dead. I guess you could say his love is one in a million."

As she bends down to retrieve the knife, I curse myself for not attempting to get the upper hand while she was empty handed. I could've grabbed something and at least tried to hit her over the head with it.

"Candace, please let me get you some help. Why don't you put the knife down and we can get someone to—"

Shaking her head, she yelled, "No, Brittain, you don't get to feel sorry for me. You must be held accountable for your part in this. You killed Kenneth!"

I waved my hands. "Excuse me, no, ma'am. I didn't have anything to do with your psychotic episode." I exhaled, not wanting to escalate the matter anymore than it was. I stepped back to distance myself from her.

"You basically put the knife in my hands when you decided you didn't want to be with him. It's your fault. Your. Fault. *Your fault!*"

She dove toward me with the knife. I grabbed her hands, trying to protect myself. She was petite, but crazy strong. In the struggle, we slammed against the wall in the hallway, knocking a picture off the wall and sending the coat-rack down with a thud.

"Drop the weapon and put your hands above your head," Elias ordered.

Candace loosened her grip on my wrist as she whipped around to see Elias standing in the kitchen entrance with his gun drawn and his police badge for her to see he meant business.

"Ha! So this is why you couldn't bother to get back with Kenneth? You were already shagging someone new. You selfish little whore," she grunted, pointing at me with the knife.

"Ma'am, I'm only going to warn you once more. Drop the weapon," he ordered.

This time, Candace did as she was told, and I rushed to kick the knife in the direction where Elias was standing.

"Britt, you good?" he asked, never moving his eyes from her.

I nodded, unable to speak. My eyes remained on Candace as Elias walked over with his gun aimed at her. Once he grabbed Candace's arms and secured them behind her back, I exhaled.

"As soon as I saw her at your door, I went ahead and put a call in," Elias said. "Luckily, they were in route to ask you a few questions since you were among the last of the incoming and outgoing calls in Mr. Wallace's phone log."

Minutes later, I looked up to see flashing lights and hear the wail of sirens outside of the house, which caused my shoulders to relax. I needed closure on Kenneth, but this, for darn sure, wasn't how I expected to receive it.

As the police detained Candace, she didn't even bother to fight them. She seemed void of any emotions. After watching them put her in the back of the car, I closed my eyes and shivered at the thought of what could've happened had Elias not been there. For the third time today, he'd come to my rescue.

Looking over at him talking with the officers, I was so thankful I had run into him today. Funny how God places you in situations that can change your life. In this instance, mine was spared by an old friend who just so happened to now be a detective.

I wasn't sure if a new relationship would blossom with Elias, but if I'd learned anything from the situation with Kenneth, the message would definitely be proceed with caution. 'Cause love can have crazy consequences if you don't watch your step.

CHAPTER SIXTEEN

DARREN

PULLING in front of the high-rise condominium, I thought I would be the one making a surprise appearance, but I was the one with my mouth hanging open, wondering why there were several police cars and residents standing outside of the building.

I approached slowly and then began to jog toward the area the police had blocked off.

"What's going on?" I questioned some of the onlookers.

"I don't really know. One dead and one who looked pretty beat up as far as I could see, but I'm not sure what exactly happened."

I looked around the lot, but didn't see Trish's car anywhere. The phone tracker brought me here, so she had to be close.

"Excuse me, sorry, but is this the only place to park for this building?"

"No, there's a parking garage around the back."

I circled around the back and tried to get to the deck, but of course, the police had that blocked off as well. Getting nowhere, I stood behind the barricade, as EMT's emerged, pushing out gurneys. One with the victim covered in an ominous white sheet, and the other was Trish. Slipping past an officer, I raced toward her.

"Trish! Trish!" I shouted.

"Get back, sir, you have to get back," one of the officers commanded, while trying to detain me.

"Let me go, please. Please, my wife…that's my wife," I shouted, wrestling free of the two officers holding me.

She wasn't conscious, but her not being covered gave me hope she was still alive.

"Were you able to get anything from her on what happened?" I asked one of the EMT's.

"No, sir, she was out when we arrived."

I scanned the crowd. I didn't see Zach. I knew it was wrong to wish the worst even on someone I despised, but I really hoped he was the one heading to the morgue if he had done this to Trish.

"The deceased – was it a Zachary Hollister?"

"The victim was female, sir. You'll have to move out of the way or you can get in to escort your wife to the hospital."

Looking down at Trish, I saw her eyes fluttering. "Ren, Ren," Trish managed. "He tried…he tried to ki- kill me. I got him…I got him."

"Trish, what have you gotten yourself into?" I ran my hands through her hair that was matted with blood.

"Zach. Tell them. It was Zach. He… I don't know where he went," she murmured before drifting off again.

"Please get her to the hospital. I want to talk to the police. I'll be by to see you." I kissed her on the forehead, got the hospital location from the EMT, and then headed over to one of the detectives taking information.

I pushed through the crowd, my mind racing with malicious thoughts.

"Where you at, you sick bastard?" I mumbled to myself.

Combing through the bystanders, I didn't have to wait long to locate Zach. The police had him pinned to the ground. His luxury vehicle was now intertwined with a tree. He was no doubt trying to flee the scene, but the police caught him before he got away. His pretty boy looks were now decorated in scratches and cuts. Looked like Trish had fought for her life. Those self-defense classes paid off.

I attempted to get closer, once again being blocked.

"Sir, you need to stand back."

"That man tried to kill my wife, Trish. Trish Morrison. She's the one that survived. That's Zachary Hollister, my wife's boss," I say, choosing to omit that he was her lover, too. "I want to make sure he's charged to the fullest extent."

The officer peered over his shoulder. "The neighbor ID'd. Don't worry. We've been looking for him for a while."

"What do you mean by that?"

"Mr. Hollister has been on a bit of a killing spree. Preying on young girls on those sugar daddy dating sites. He usually prefers those that are unattached. Makes it easier to kill and flee without anyone looking into their disappearance."

"How was he getting the bodies out undiscovered all this time?" I asked. I couldn't wrap my head around how this guy was a serial killer in a condominium and it went unnoticed.

"He traveled a lot for business, but at times those suitcases weren't filled with clothes. He typically drugged his victims, which is why no one ever heard a lot of ruckus from his place. He did some pretty gruesome things." He frowned and shook his head. "Your wife is lucky the neighbor called to report a disturbance. Had she not been proactive, your wife might not have survived the attack."

My blood boiled as I stared at Zachary's emotionless face. His eyes smiled, but behind those eyes, he was vacant. My wife thought she'd be happier here. Somehow, he'd painted that image for her and Lord knows how many other defenseless souls.

No longer able to look at the pieces of the broken man that sat before me, I turned to get back to my car and to my wife. Though our relationship was tattered, I knew the moment I walked into that hospital, I wasn't planning to leave her side. For as long as she'd let me, I planned to be her husband, come what may.

CHAPTER SEVENTEEN

HEIDI

MY ARMS BEGAN to ache as I held them in place. We were at a silent standoff. I wanted to protest and attempt to get myself and the girls to safety. I was trying my best to keep still. I didn't trust that those two little girls wouldn't twitch and make noises, fearing the recognizable voices rising through the ceiling.

"Suzie, I got this under control. Why don't you just head back to the car?"

I flinched as she pushed me down to the floor. "No way, Pat. If you had this under control, your girl wouldn't have found the merchandise. How long have you known about it, Heidi? Is that the real reason you put my brother out?"

"I just found the DVDs today when I was trying to find umm, a hammer to hang some pictures I had in the garage."

Patrick looked over to the entryway from the garage and saw the artwork I'd purchased at a farmer's market a month ago. I'd been begging him to hang them up, but he never got around to it. It was a quick lie, but worked considering the circumstances.

"That checks out. She's been trying to get those paintings up for a minute. But that doesn't excuse the fact that you started snooping. The toolbox is locked. You should've just waited until I returned home."

Again, he had a lot of her nerve to try to have some authority here, but there was the fact that his sister had a gun pointed at my head.

"Pat, I think you've talked enough. The point is she knows way more than she should. If you need to leave, please go right ahead, but I'm finishing her off. We can't have any witnesses."

Patrick approached slowly, both of his hands raised. It was clear he was just as afraid of his sister as I was right now.

"Heidi knows better than to go against me. She knows she messed up putting me out of the house, and I'm sure she wouldn't create any drama for us. She's gonna be a good girl and do what's best for the family. Right, Heidi?"

Brows raised, I had a brief moment of memory loss and thought to curse him out, but looking up at Suzanne aiming the gun at my face put things into perspective quickly.

"Patrick, you can have the house and your secrets. Just don't hurt me."

Suzanne began laughing manically. "Oh, stop it. That performance was worse than any I've seen on reality television. You know good and well that as soon as we let you go, you're off to the police. That can't happen. I'm sorry, Heidi. Any last words?"

I blinked and started shooting questions. "Was Patrick the mastermind behind this? Were you in any of those videos? How long has this been going on?"

Patrick held up his hands. "No. I only stored the movies here and sold them through the website. I didn't handle the cash or solicit the girls."

"Patrick, you've said more than enough. Shut up, or I'll shoot you once I'm done with her."

Patrick shook his head. "No, Suzie, this has gone on long

enough. We can stop and start over. We don't have to keep doing this."

The curse words Suzanne spat indicated the turn in the room. We'd officially gone from bad to worse. "You're pissing me off, Pat. Now look, start breaking some things around the house. We'll make this look like a robbery, frame her for the videos, and be on our merry way. That's how we get to start over. Her being free to talk is not an option."

"Well, if anyone is going to kill her, it should be me. She's my wife. It should be someone she loves," Patrick said, getting closer and reaching for the gun.

I twisted my lips. I wasn't sure if this was his attempt at one last romantic gesture, but I guess him behind the gun might be less terrifying than the thought of his crazy sister holding it.

Suzanne shrugged. "I guess you deserve to get in a shot, but I'll finish her off." Just as she was preparing to pass the gun, something caused her to pause. She glared down at me. "I guess you're a better liar than I thought. Almost got away with it, too."

Following her gaze at the mirror, I looked over my shoulder to see the girls peeking from the top of the stairs. Patrick noticed, too, and shook his head.

"Heidi, why did you bring them here? What were you thinking?"

"I found them in the shed. They were already here," I said through gritted teeth.

Patrick shook his head. "Now you're making up stuff. There's nothing in that shed but junk."

"Get your tails down here and lay down on the floor with your *hero*," Suzanne yelled.

"Suz, what's Heidi talking about?" Patrick questioned. "She's making that up, right?"

Rolling her eyes, Suzanne turned the gun on Patrick. "Shut up before I have you join them. The less you know the better."

His eyes bulged and he cursed. "You kept them here? How many are there?"

"Shut up, you idiot!" Suzanne barked. She inhaled. "Now, find something to tie them up, while I think of what to do next."

"Wha—what do you mean? They are just kids. You can't... this has gone far enough."

Suzanne cackled. "Let me get this straight. Are you saying to let them all go? Including your wife, and expect this not to come back on me? Pathetic."

Patrick ran his hands through his hair and cursed before lunging forward at Suzanne. I watched in horror as he pushed her hand toward the ceiling. One single shot rang out, hitting the light fixture. The two fell to the ground and tussled. I took it as an opportunity to get the girls out.

"Girls, run and get help," I screamed. They hesitated, but soon got over their shock and ran out the door. I crouched down and started to run in the opposite direction of Patrick and Suzanne fighting, and made it toward the back door when I heard another shot. I froze in place, sure I would be next.

"Hei—Heidi."

Recognizing Patrick's voice, I turned back in his direction. He was the shooter. In front of him lay Suzanne in a pool of blood. One shot to the chest and one in the arm.

"Is she dead?" he quizzed.

I walked over and checked her pulse. It was weak, but she was still alive. "No, she's alive." I say, looking over my shoulder at him.

Patrick's body shook as he held the gun against his temple.

"Patrick, what are you doing?"

"I can't go to jail. They'll kill me in there, Heidi. I didn't know she held those girls captive. I didn't, but no one is going to believe that."

I could hear the faint sound of sirens in the distance. I tried to keep him talking. "How did you get involved in this if you're saying you didn't really know the details?"

"Suzanne had to bail me out. I had gotten involved in some sketchy business and lost all of our money. She gave me a loan, pending I let her store her product here. I agreed without knowing what that was. But I swear, once I knew what was going on, I tried to get out of it."

I shook my head. "I wish I could believe you about wanting out, but you should have just reported her to the police. And now you've put yourself in this mess – both of us – in this mess. You shouldn't have come back here today. This could've been avoided."

"Maybe. We won't know because Suzanne knew you'd snitch if you found out."

I nodded. "I just wanted to start over. I didn't anticipate any of this. I never would have thought you could do anything like this."

"And I didn't. I didn't want to be in this. I can't let the police take me away. I can't go to jail knowing I'm only guilty of being bullied into this life. Bye, Heidi. I love you."

"Patrick, nooooo," I screamed.

I winced as the bullet penetrated his skull, pushing out all our memories, all his troubles, and his final thoughts of being free, all over the white walls. The walls, which housed our memories—wedding photos, vacation getaways, awards and accolades—were now covered with new memories of the day I found out my husband sold child pornography and the last day I would call this place home.

"Heidi!" my cousin Vance yelled, running over to my side. "Jesus, what happened in here? Are you all right? What the hell happened?"

"Oh Vance, it was so awful." I grabbed my head and squeezed my eyes tight.

I looked up to see the police running through the door.

"Who…did you call the police?" I asked.

He nodded. "I tried calling you several times on my way over here. When I didn't hear back from you, I got worried and called the police. Are you okay? What did I just walk into?"

I turned and fell into his arms. My tears deepened as more police officers came into the room. "I'll let you catch it on the news. All I want now is to get far away from this house."

Vance squeezed my shoulders. "Yeah, we can get you out of here. You can stay with me as long as you need."

I gasped. "The girls…there were two little girls."

"Don't worry. When I arrived, they were standing outside with a neighbor."

I groaned. "What they must think of me. I definitely can't continue living here."

"You can come stay with me until I can get the house cleaned up for you."

I shook my head. "No, it's time to move. Go somewhere and start fresh."

Vance nodded. "Ready to be interrogated?"

"If it means closing out this chapter, absolutely," I replied.

Looking at Patrick slumped over in the bay window, the same place where we shared so many hopes and dreams, I ached inside. Once again, we had conversed on our desires for the future – mine to start over and his to be free.

Thank you and I hope you enjoyed reading, Kissing Strangers: Tainted Love

Continue reading for an excerpt from my debut novel, Truth Is…

NOW AVAILABLE

PROLOGUE

ANSLEY STARED over at her laptop, wringing her hands together; her curiosity nagging at her. Could everything she ever wanted to know about a guy be right at her finger tips?

She rose from the sofa and walked over to the makeshift office she created in her condo by the window. Lowering herself in the chair, she left clicked on the mouse to bring her purveyor of the truth to life. Or at least she aspired to find some hidden truths.

The cat and mouse game she was playing in her head right now was borderline manic. She wasn't sure if she should research Davis. After all, she wouldn't want him Googling her, but then again she had nothing to hide. And in reality, researching a potential love interest was a given now-a-days when it came to meeting someone new.

As far as Ansley was concerned, Davis had led her down this road of suspicion. Besides, if he wasn't so obscure, she wouldn't have to play catfish detective.

Guilt began to settle in. This wasn't right. Or was it?

"Okay enough back and forth, it's go time," she said aloud. She took a deep breath and keyed in the link for Don't Date Him Girl.com.

Ansley felt a twinge of sadness consume her. This was disappointing to her that dating now required a keen sense of snooping or a thorough background check.

She located the search bar on her screen, and entered the name Davis Montclair. She was impressed at how thorough the site seemed to be—it was her very own Angela Lansbury.

As she watched the waiting wheel spinning, letting her know that her laptop was searching for information, Ansley got up from her chair and walked over to the refrigerator.

"I don't know why I was planning to do this without wine. Sleuthing deserves at least a glass," she said to herself.

Pouring her merlot to the rim, Ansley took a quick sip and turned back towards her desk. She held her glass as if it was her life source, gripping the stem a little tighter than required. Ansley took another sip, which turned into a gulp. With a slight turn of her body, Ansley reached over and grabbed the wine bottle from the island.

Who knows what was waiting for her on that screen.

Returning to her seat, Ansley took a deep breath before hitting the space key to wake her laptop from its quick siesta. She shuddered inward at the numerous entries awaiting her. She wasn't sure if any or all would share a tale about the man attempting to woo her, but she wasn't leaving this screen until she got some answers.

She scrolled and scrolled until she found one submission that listed Davis Montclair, but as an alias and the frequented cities of Atlanta and Chicago.

This got her attention.

No turning back now, Ansley thought as she clicked on the link.

Her eyes shifted from one horrific line to the next. She didn't want to believe it was him, but once she got to the last section her heart dropped.

There right in front of her, was a photo of Davis Montclair with the woman who claimed he scorned her. She read over the entry again, just as stunned as she was upon reading it the first time.

She was confused and hurt. This man described here was not the man she was getting to know—the man who initially stood a great chance of winning her heart.

As a single tear escaped her, Ansley was left sitting with unanswered questions. She whispered, "Who are you?"

CHAPTER ONE

ANSLEY, I'm sorry but we're going to have to let you go," said Robin Barnett, the Editor-in-Chief of New Breed Publishing and the grim reaper of Ansley's livelihood. Sitting in Robin's office, she tried to maintain her composure. Her foot tapped against the plush carpet, unbeknownst to the self-absorbed, narcissist sitting across from her. "You really don't have the…voice… that appeals to our readers."

New Breed Publishing produced Atlanta Urbane, one of the hottest e-magazines in the city, spotlighting young entrepreneurs, entertainers, authors and the Who's who of Atlanta. Ansley was fortunate enough to become a feature writer, getting into the industry straight out of college.

Ansley thought the concept for the e-magazine was edgy and progressive; it was the voice of her generation. Unfortunately, she joined the team during the midst of the Robin era. Quincy Barnett left the company in his daughter's incapable hands while trying to expand the brand to other cities.

In Ansley's opinion, Robin was driving the company into the ground. It would not surprise her if the publication shut down before she made it to the unemployment office. Robin was a wanna-be-fashionista who seriously needed a class on how to dress when coming to work. Her provocative attire always screamed happy hour. Ansley recalled one of Robin's most infamous outfits, a sheer white top with a lacy bra and some barely there shorts. It was not a surprise to anyone though, workplace rules never applied to Robin. She did as she pleased.

"I understand. It's business—not personal, right?" Ansley said, leaning back against in her seat, her stance becoming more defensive by the minute. She knew Robin was not very fond of her. Not that she would say that to her directly.

Robin took a breath and batted her poorly applied eyelash extensions. "The department is going in another direction, and… if I'm being honest, I don't see how you fit in... I'm just not a fan. Do you have any questions?"

She stood up and shook her head at Robin's curt response. "No, I think I'm all set here."

Robin gave her a fake smile. "Well, take care…oh and if I don't see you, happy New Year."

Ansley sent a sharp glare in Robin's direction before walking out of the office. Just as she got to the doorway, she heard the witch utter, "And that's how it's done."

"Girl, you are brutal. I couldn't work for you," Ansley heard another voice say.

"Umm—excuse me, did you have a third party in our conversation?" Ansley stepped back into the office and toward Robin's desk. Noticing that the phone was on speaker, she stood with her hands planted on her hips as she waited for a response.

"It's very rude to eavesdrop. Besides it's only my girl, Roxy."

"Roxy, as in Roxanne the office gossip in marketing? Wow," Ansley took a calming breath. "You know what? I'm not even gonna let you take me there."

She took the phone off speaker and disconnected the call.

Robin gasped. "Excuse me…"

"I wish I could …"

Robin lifted her right hand and shooed Ansley out the door.

Robin had been anti-Ansley from the start and it was all because Robin's father, Quincy had been her biggest supporter. He was a visionary and tried to help everyone find that best version of him or herself. After observing her work ethic, he offered to become her mentor. She felt that Robin was jealous early on and knew that she would take the first opportunity to cut her loose.

Ansley reminded herself that her dreams were greater than this company, but with less than a year as an established journalist, she would have to rejoin the large number of nameless writers in the industry unknown—faceless and voiceless.

While Ansley was grateful to have gotten the opportunity, she couldn't stop thinking on how she had sacrificed love for a limited position that did not escalate her career to the height she desired. If she knew then what she was learning now, she would have focused more in the direction of her relationship with Ryan, but she was afraid to put all of herself into that relationship when she still had dreams unfulfilled. Not willing to go all in…at least not the way Ryan described, she let him go. Now she was left with regret, wishing she had him to lean on.

She went to her cubicle, gathered her personal belongings and walked toward the exit. There was nothing left for her here, but there was much to anticipate in the city. At least she hoped so.

Fired from a job the day before New Year's Eve was not anything she anticipated happening. She certainly had not planned to spend the coming year looking for a job. Ansley wanted to be the bigger person—she wanted to feel gratitude that they waited until the end of December to let her go, but her mind could only process the negative.

Once she settled inside her car, she pulled out her phone to call Simeon, one of her best friends.

"Simeon Harris speaking," she said in her heavy Southern drawl.

Ansley could hear the click of Simeon's nails against the keyboard. Simeon was a Marketing Executive with the Bloomquist Corporation. "Hey lady. What you got going for the rest of the day? I need to grab lunch, and by lunch…I mean I need a drink."

"Oh goodness," Simeon said. "What did she do?"

"You know how Robin makes it her business to belittle my work daily. Trying to tell me that I can't relate to our African American readership…well, she finally decided to stop toying with me and executed the final blow."

Robin's words were a slap in the face to Ansley, as she was African American, and very in touch with the community as compared to Robin, who would only take a stand for a sale at Saks.

Simeon's sigh was audible. "I'm so sorry, girl. Where do you want to meet?"

"The usual spot is fine… I'll be two drinks ahead of you," Ansley said.

One hour later, Ansley waved to Simeon when she spotted her sashay through the doors of Tin Lizzy's. The stares of admiration and lust by the male patrons didn't cause Simeon to react at all. She was accustomed to being the focal point of every man in the room. Simeon wore her raven black hair in a long, layered bob, which complemented her deep mocha complexion. She was beautiful, intelligent, and possessed an extremely fit physique. She had even tried to help Ansley get a more sculpted body, but her friend did not want to be bound to a meal plan. Ansley complained that it felt unnatural.

"Okay sweetie. Let's snap you out of this emotional pothole. I could see that frown clear across the room," Simeon said, as she sat down across from Ansley. "Have you had a chance to think about what you would want to do next?"

"Right before they dropped the bomb on me, I had just enrolled in an online master's degree program," Ansley stated. "I'm debating on whether or not I should move forward."

"Think about it before you make an impulsive decision," Simeon advised. "What about your manuscript? Didn't you say you had started working on a project?"

Ansley frowned. "I haven't touched that thing in years."

"Well, just sit down and let the characters tell you the story. It'll come to you, or so they say," Simeon responded, repeating something she'd probably heard an author say at a book signing.

Ansley shrugged off Simeon's sentiments. Every dream that Ansley had for her life after college included writing. She wanted to be a feature writer for the Atlanta Journal Constitution, and release some reference books for journalism students on how to find internships and plot out a career path. That was her passion. She attempted to write fiction as well, but that project was now collecting dust with the rest of her textbooks.

"Hey, it was just a suggestion. As far as the job is concerned, I have some contacts, so I'll make a few calls and see if I can generate some leads for you."

"Thanks girl," Ansley responded. "I won't turn down your offer. I know you have connections." She paused a moment before saying, "What's going on with you? Give me some good news."

"Work has been crazy these past few weeks," Simeon responded. "But the New Year's Eve party tomorrow night will be the perfect way to close out the week. Oh, and don't forget you're my plus one. I'll understand if you want to back out, but I hope you won't because we've had this planned for a while now. And I'm not trying to hear that, I don't have anything to wear mess either."

Simeon settled back against the cushion of her seat.

Ansley could tell by her friend's body language that she was mentally preparing for a letdown. The raised brow and crossed arms were a big clue of Simeon's current disposition.

"I'm not really in the mood to party, but I did promise that I'd go. I'm not sure how much fun I'm going to be though."

"We're going to have a great time. This is exactly what you need to lift your spirits, trust. It's going to be all the way turnt up."

As if on cue, Levon, their favorite waiter came to the table with their usual order. "Okay dolls, I have a pitcher of Peach Patron Margaritas and the barbecue chicken and goat cheese quesadillas for two," he said.

Ansley and Simeon were regulars at Tin Lizzy's. It was their safe haven and the place where they first met. It was just three months ago that the two of them met at the bar while sitting and complaining about their horrible bosses. They became fast friends after bonding over margaritas and the Tex-Mex cuisine. They went from grabbing an occasional drink for networking purposes to dining there two to three times a week, it was like their own version of the television show, Cheers. Everyone knew their names and on occasion, they would get the royal treatment, which meant the manager comped meals for them.

"These drinks are everything to me right now," Ansley said with a little too much enthusiasm.

Simeon took a sip. "Their drinks stay on point."

Ansley nodded and sighed. Even her favorite drink wasn't giving her the instant boost she needed. Simeon noticed and patted Ansley's hand.

"It will all work out. Now eat your half. I can't promise that I won't try to put my fork on your side."

They continued to chat for a while as they ate their meal, but

Ansley was getting tired of faking it. All she wanted to do was go home, take a warm bath, and get in the bed.

"Thanks for coming out. I really appreciate you being there for me."

"You would do the same for me. It's not a problem."

"I hate to eat and run, but I think I'm going to go ahead and make my way to the house."

Ansley rose and Simeon stood as well to say goodbye.

"Let me know when you get home. I'm gonna finish our drinks." Simeon's smile was full of mischief.

"Levon," Ansley called. "Make sure she's not stumbling out of here." Once he gave her a thumbs up, Ansley was on her way out the door.

Outside, Ansley fumbled around in her purse searching for her keys as she walked. She was not paying attention to where she was going, which caused her to literally fall into a pair of masculine arms.

"Excuse me, I'm so sorry," she said, looking up at the man.

As he helped steady her, Ansley casted her eyes away from him, unable to hide her emotions. After all these years, seeing him still made her heart beat overtime.

She found her voice. "Oh wow... Ryan." She allowed herself to sneak another glimpse at him. How he managed to become even more handsome after all these years, she shook her head. "You look—amazing."

Ryan Bennett was her college sweetheart. He had always been attractive and adulthood really agreed with him. He was tall, 6 feet and 5 inches of solid, sexy caramel, built, well-groomed and full of never-ending, glory-halle-stupid, fine. His brown sugar sprinkled eyes were always warm and welcoming, and he had the longest eyelashes that Maybelline Cosmetics would no doubt want to bottle up and sell. She could kick herself for giving up their relationship.

He looked at her and smiled briefly.

"Hey Ans..." he said. "You're just as beautiful as ever."

Ansley blushed and mouthed, "Thank you."

"Is everything okay? Based on our collision, I can only assume you were a little distracted."

She felt a little gratification that he was taking the time to check on her. Up until that moment, Ansley had barely acknowledged the woman hovering to Ryan's right. She seemed all too bothered about this unanticipated reunion.

"Oh, that," she chuckled. "I was trying to find my keys when I ran into you. I'm okay though. Just got some disappointing news, but other than that I'm doing okay."

"So what's the bad news? Do you want to talk about it? I can give you a call later if you want."

"Well... um, it's nothing major. I just need to get home, take a long shower, and relax to some jazz or something. Look, I don't want to hold you up...so," she said, looking at his date, who was now tapping her foot.

"Oh! My bad... sorry about that. Ansley, this is my friend from work... umm..."

"Nina. My name is Nina."

"Just like in Love Jones. Nice to meet you," Ansley greeted. "That was one of our favorite movies in college. Right, Ryan?"

"Oh yeah," Ryan chuckled. "I didn't even think about that. I use to love me some Nia Long, still do—a blues for Nina." Ryan shook his head. "Anyway, Nina, this is my Ansley... I mean this is Ansley," he said with a nervous laugh.

Nina sneered at Ansley.

"Ryan... can we go somewhere else to eat? It looks too crowded and a little low brow here," she said, rolling her eyes in Ansley's direction.

Ansley laughed and shook her head. The way his coworker was acting—she must have thought she and Ryan were on a date.

Whatever the case, she didn't intend to get into an altercation with this woman over her ex. It just didn't make sense to go there.

"Ansley, give me a call if you want to talk about whatever is bothering you... or if you just want to catch up," he said before walking away. Ansley wondered how he managed to walk with Nina so close alongside him as if they were participating in a three-legged race.

As she stood there watching them disappear around the corner, she recalled a time when it was her and Ryan that were inseparable. They walked to class together. They always made time for each other—or at least until she started to lose sight of their relationship. She thought about the night that changed everything.

Ansley and Ryan sat on the floor of his apartment, eating pizza and watching Love Jones. It was their movie.

Ansley reached over to grab some popcorn, and noticed that Ryan was watching her and not the movie. She smiled. "I see someone is not watching the movie. What's on your mind?

Ryan grabbed the remote from behind him on the sofa, and pressed the pause button. He turned his head in Ansley's direction.

"Ansley, we are about to graduate in a few months. Can you believe it's already been four years?"

"I know right. I was looking through photos from freshman year the other day, and just seeing how much I've changed. You too," she reached over and patted Ryan's evidence of the freshman fifteen.

"Oh you trying to be funny. That's alright though, you don't have to love my something extra," he said before reaching over to caress her thick thighs. "I love my baby's curves and lady lumps. You still freshman year sexy. I'll give it to you."

They laughed together. As Ryan turned the rest of his body in her direction, Ansley also adjusted her body so that she could face him.

She smiled at him. Ansley loved Ryan. She never thought that she could love someone they way that she loved him. She noticed the shift in his mood, and braced herself.

"I've been waiting until we got together tonight to share something with you," he said fiddling with the edges of the pizza box that rest between them.

Ansley wanted to interject and make him rush the information, but she remained quiet and waited to see what he would say next.

"I wanted to let you know that I got offered a position as a Financial Analyst with American Express."

"Oh my gosh. Ryan, that's incredible. So where will your office be? I hope they put you in the Atlanta office, the commute to Lawrenceville would tack on some extra miles for you. Give me a kiss, a hug or something. We need to celebrate."

She crawled across the floor to get closer to him. They shared a kiss, a lackluster kiss if Ansley was to tell it.

"Ryan baby, that kiss was a little bland. Are you nervous? You have a while before you start, or are they starting you early?"

"It's in New York. I'll be moving up north and I want you to join me. Ansley Renee Wright, I can't imagine starting this journey without you. I know I don't have a ring right now, but will you marry me?"

Relocating with him meant giving up her dream to write for the Atlanta Journal Constitution. However, Ryan just didn't understand why she didn't want to work for the Wall Street Journal or New York Times, which frustrated her. Now here she stood, jobless and nowhere near getting a call from the AJC. Every submission she submitted had been declined or unanswered.

Coming back to present, Ansley wished she had a do over, she would be his wife and she would've found her way into the industry, or freelanced, but she would have made it happen. Back then, she failed to realize that her passion wasn't based on her home address, it was based on where it lived inside of her.

No job. Seeing an ex and he looks to be winning. Yet he still showed concern for her—when reality checked in, it was prompt and painful.

It was official. Today totally sucked.

———

SIMEON RAN her fingers through her hair; the ends always seemed to get a little tangled when she did wand curls. She refreshed her lip-gloss, and gazed around the restaurant as she waited to settle her bill. When Levon returned to the table with her debit card, he also brought her a message.

"Miss Simeon, the gentleman at the bar has taken care of your bill." Levon pointed. "The one in the tweed blazer, and wearing those anointed, take-me-to-the-king pants. Yes, yes, honey. Don't keep him waiting."

Simeon burst out laughing. "You know you need to cut it out."

She adjusted her body to get a better look. Liking what she saw, she smiled and allowed her tongue to tease the corner of her mouth as she recalled the last time she laid eyes on this fine specimen at the bar.

She returned her card to the clutch she carried, and walked over towards the bar to extend her thanks. By the way he leaned back against the bar drinking in her frame, Simeon could tell the energy that she felt upon sight was mutual.

"Montgomery, well isn't this a pleasant surprise. What are you doing in Georgia?"

As he reached around her waist, pulling her close for a hug, Simeon's body temperature elevated, right along with her desire for him. They had history; one that she hoped they could rekindle and put on repeat forever.

She met him a few months ago while attending a conference in Chicago on marketing and social media. He was attending a conference in the same hotel. They struck up a conversation over drinks in the restaurant's bar lounge area. As far as Simeon was concerned, their business was far from over.

She inhaled his scent, the familiarity of lavender and oak enticed her senses. She had instant recall of this fragrance, but couldn't recall the name of the cologne. Simeon was so consumed with remembering the name, she almost missed his response to her query.

"I came to Georgia to help my cousin with some projects and decided to take on a contract position while I'm down here."

"Wait, are you saying you quit your job in Chicago?" Simeon inquired.

"No. Not yet. I'm just down here to test the waters. You know I never got your number. You were a hard woman to track down."

Simeon tilted her head and smiled. "Not buying into that real estate of lies. I gave you a card."

He shook his head and shrugged. "I got a lot of cards at that conference. I couldn't recall your name—I never said I was Colombo, but I'm here now, so why don't you have another drink with me. Maybe we can pick up where we left off?"

He grazed her breast with his hand.

"Seriously? That's the best you can come up with?" Simeon turned away, and began to walk towards the exit. She wasn't about the let him treat her like some tramp. She deserved better.

Her face flush, and jaws clenched. She attempted to calm her nerves by inhaling and exhaling out her negative thoughts, but with each step she could not fight how she felt—she was simmering hot. She couldn't believe that he had hope to run into her, but only for a quickie. They shared a romantic evening, albeit a one night stand, but this was not normally her style. It also bothered her that he never called after that night. She didn't even get a Facebook request. However, she never bothered to reach out to him either.

"Simeon wait," he said, walking briskly to catch up with her. "I'm sorry. You're a beautiful woman and that night, wow—it was special to me, too. At the time though, as you may recall I was going through some things with my ex-girlfriend. As soon as I came to town, I decided to look you up. I remembered you talking about this place so I chanced it. It's fate."

"So you're telling me that this is not just an attempt to get me back into bed." Lowering her voice, Simeon stated, "I'm nobody's jump-off."

"I know that. Look, I think we should get to know one another better. We can start by having lunch later this week."

Simeon's eyes lit up and she clapped her hands. "I'd love it."

She wanted him as much as he wanted her. The night they spent together had been spectacular. It had been automatic, explosions of desire. Her body gave a tiny shudder just at the memory of what they had shared.

Simeon began to dance in place humming the song Automatic by The Pointer Sisters. She noticed that Davis was giving her a peculiar look, and noted that she needed to not scare him away. She needed to welcome him back to the comfort zone that she had established in Chicago.

She winked at him, turning to walk back toward the exit. Stealing a peek over her shoulder, Simeon asked, "Aren't you coming?"

He smiled as she took his hand leading the way, as Simeon continued to hum The Pointer's Sister song, *Automatic* in her head.

Made in the
USA
Middletown, DE